ANNETTE BROADRICK

Come Be My Love

Published by Silhouette Books New York

America's Publisher of Contemporary Romance

This book is dedicated to fellow writers Noreen
Brownlie and Susan Naomi Horton whose long-
distance encouragement and assistance in plotting
and planning not only helped me to hang on to my
sanity but also contributed to the increased revenues
of the telephone companies for two nations!

Thank you both for your beautiful friendships. I
have been doubly blessed.

SILHOUETTE BOOKS
300 E. 42nd St., New York, N.Y. 10017

Copyright © 1988 by Annette Broadrick

ISBN: 0-373-08609-1

First Silhouette Books printing October 1988

"You're a very private man,"

Brandi said.

Greg gave her comment some thought. "I suppose I am."

"And yet you've been very open with me," she pointed out.

"You have that effect on me. I don't understand it, nor can I explain it."

"I'm glad, Greg," she said softly. Leaning toward him, she kissed him gently on the cheek.

He turned, pulled her into his lap and looked down at her in his arms. "This is a dangerous situation, you know," he said slowly. "One of us needs to hang on to his sanity."

She smiled and stroked his cheek. "What a sensible idea. Should we draw straws and see who wins?"

"And the winner keeps his sanity?"

She touched her lips to his for a brief instant. "No. The loser."

Dear Reader:

The spirit of the Silhouette Romance Homecoming Celebration lives on as each month we bring you six books by continuing stars!

And there are some wonderful stories in the stars for you. During the coming months, we're publishing romances by many of your favorite authors, including Brittany Young, Lucy Gordon and Rita Rainville. In addition, we have some very special treats planned for the fall and winter of 1988.

In October, watch for *Tyler*—Book III of Diana Palmer's exciting trilogy, Long, Tall Texans. Diana's handsome Tyler is sure to lasso your heart—forever!

Also in October is Annette Broadrick's *Come Be My Love*—the exciting sequel to *That's What Friends Are For*. Remember Greg Duncan, the mysterious bridegroom? Well, sparks fly when he meets his match—Brandi Martin!

And Sal Giordiano, the handsome detective featured in *Sherlock's Home* by Sharon De Vita, is returning in November with his own story—*Italian Knights*.

There's plenty more for you to discover in the Silhouette Romance line during the fall and winter. So as the weather turns colder, enjoy the warmth of love while you are reading Silhouette Romances. Your response to these authors and other authors of Silhouette Romances has served as a touchstone for us, and we're pleased to bring you more books with Silhouette's distinctive medley of charm, wit and— above all—*romance*.

I hope you enjoy this book and the many stories to come. Come home to Silhouette Romance—for always!

Sincerely,

Tara Hughes
Senior Editor
Silhouette Books

Books by Annette Broadrick

Silhouette Romance

Circumstantial Evidence #329
Provocative Peril #359
Sound of Summer #412
Unheavenly Angel #442
Strange Enchantment #501
Mystery Lover #533
That's What Friends Are For #544
Come Be My Love #609

Silhouette Desire

Hunter's Prey #185
Bachelor Father #219
Hawk's Flight #242
Deceptions #272
Choices #283
Heat of the Night #314
Made in Heaven #336
Return to Yesterday #360
Adam's Story #367
Momentary Marriage #414
With All My Heart #433

ANNETTE BROADRICK

lives on the shores of The Lake of the Ozarks in Missouri where she spends her time doing what she loves most—reading and writing romantic fiction. "For twenty-five years I lived in various large cities, working as a legal secretary, a very high-stress occupation. I never thought I was capable of making a career change at this point in my life, but thanks to Silhouette I am now able to write full-time in the peaceful surroundings that have turned my life into a dream come true."

IOWA

NEBRASKA

ILLINOIS

Payton

KANSAS ● Kansas City

Missouri River

St. Louis

MISSOURI
Underlined places are fictitious.

ARKANSAS

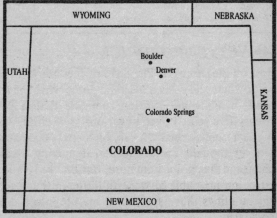

WYOMING

NEBRASKA

UTAH

Boulder
●
Denver
●

KANSAS

Colorado Springs
●

COLORADO

NEW MEXICO

Chapter One

The high beams of Gregory Duncan's headlights glimmered on the blanketing snow that weighted the branches of the evergreens surrounding Tim's A-frame chalet. The snow sparkled with a glitter that caused Greg to smile as he made the last sharp turn into the empty driveway.

He sat there for a moment, absorbing the night silence and the beauty of the heavy snow. He was looking forward to the next few days, to the solitude that he'd finally decided he needed. The long drive from eastern Missouri to the Rocky Mountains of southern Colorado had been worth the effort. Taking in the quiet serenity and beauty around him, he knew that he'd made the right decision—to escape from his busy world and enjoy the solitude of nature.

Greg climbed from the car and stretched, then reached for his bag. His skis could wait until morning. He had plenty of time now to do whatever he wanted. At the moment, sleep was his number one priority.

He felt in his pocket for the key his friend had given him years ago, right after Tim had purchased his hideaway. Thank God for a friend like Tim, Greg thought as he mounted the steps to the door. They went back a long way.

Greg had been unable to reach Tim at his Denver office when he had suddenly decided, after an unusually long jury trial, to get away for a while. Not that contacting Tim was mandatory before using the place. Tim had always insisted that Greg treat the place as his own and that he make free use of it.

Greg had half hoped that Tim might have had the same idea and be there ahead of him, but there were no other vehicles parked around the cabin.

Given Tim's business, he could be anywhere at the moment. He went to whatever part of the world he was needed in, whenever he was called. Greg was one of the few people who knew exactly what Tim did for a living and how valuable was his contribution to the safety and continued security of the country.

Tim was a very private person. Greg knew the same could be said about his own personality, which probably explained why he and Tim had been friends for so many years.

He also understood why Tim needed a place where he could retreat on occasion and why its location was a closely guarded secret from almost everyone who knew him. Greg appreciated the trust Tim had shown in him by sharing the retreat with him.

Greg let himself in by the kitchen door and flipped on a light. Everything looked ready for occupancy. Greg knew that Tim paid a couple who lived a few miles down the road to keep an eye on the place. Tim also kept it well stocked with food. Peeking into the refrigerator, Greg smiled at the plentiful supply of canned and bottled drinks.

At the moment, all Greg wanted was several hours of uninterrupted sleep. The very idea of being somewhere without a phone or an alarm clock seemed to be the height of luxury to him.

He turned out the light and made his way to the stairs by the reflection of light from the snow outside shining through the glass wall that made up the front of the A-frame home.

The place was small but fulfilled Tim's needs—as well as Greg's. The loft area was open, with a railing overlooking the main part of the house below. An oversize bed waited in the deep shadows of the room, and Greg sank onto the edge of the mattress, wearily pulling off his shoes, then unbuttoning his shirt. Within seconds he'd stripped down to his shorts, and with a sigh of anticipation he crawled under the covers.

Alone at last was his last conscious thought.

Brandi Martin slept heavily. Her exhaustion was as much emotional as physical. Yet even in her sleep she could not find any peace of mind—her subconscious filled her dreams with people who were after her. She had to get away. She had to hide, to hide before they succeeded in killing her.

A hand brushed her shoulder.

She screamed, waking herself up, and discovered that the hand touching her hadn't been part of her dream. The bedside lamp came on and a male voice said, "What the—"

Still half submerged in her dreams, Brandi found that she was in bed with a man she'd never seen before in her life.

She screamed again.

"Good God, lady! I heard you the first time. Your reaction is duly noted. Now, for hell's sake, who are you and what are you doing here?"

Brandi felt frozen with shock and fright. She watched as the tall, well-built blond man threw back the covers on his side of the bed and stood up, revealing a well-muscled physique with very little covering it. With economical movements, he pulled on a pair of jeans that were beside the bed. He turned around and stared at her, his hands resting on his hips.

All Brandi could think about was the horrible realization that somehow, someway, she had been traced to Tim's place.

"Who are you?" Her voice quavered, and she glanced quickly around the room, searching for a weapon, any weapon.

"I asked you first."

She glanced back at him nervously. If he'd come there to kill her, would he have taken off his clothes first? "What are you doing here?" she asked, trying to fight the horror of wondering who he might be.

"What the hell does it look like, lady?" Greg ran his hand through his hair. "If you were expecting Tim, I'm sorry to disappoint you." He glanced around the room. "Where is he, anyway?"

Hearing a name that she knew caused Brandi to draw her first deep breath since she'd been jolted awake. Her heart was pounding relentlessly in her chest, and she forced herself to try to calm down. Even though she didn't know who this man was, he obviously knew Tim, which meant that he couldn't be one of the faceless men who had been pursuing her for the past three nightmarish days and nights.

She spoke her relief out loud. "You must be a friend of Tim's," she murmured, trying to calm down.

Greg sighed and sank onto the edge of the bed. Whoever this woman was, he didn't give her much in the way of brainpower. Either that or she wasn't too swift when she first awoke.

Then again, having some strange female screech in his ear wasn't his idea of a great good-morning call, either. He glanced at his watch in disgust. He'd driven fourteen hours, hadn't gotten to sleep until two, and now it was barely five in the morning.

Greg studied the woman in the bed closely, wondering who she was and how she'd managed to get inside Tim's cabin. He knew he'd never seen her before. He would have remembered her. She was small, with short black curls that reminded him of a baby's fine hair falling over her forehead and feathering around her ears and the nape of her neck. Her eyes, a prominent feature in her elfin face, were so deeply blue they looked almost black in the lamplight, with lashes so thick that they appeared to be smudges that made her large eyes seem even larger. At the moment she was very pale, but Greg guessed that her skin was naturally fair.

She inched back against the headboard as though she were afraid of him when he sat down on the bed. Greg found her attitude ludicrous, but at the moment he could think of no way to reassure her that he didn't make a practice of attacking women—and particularly not at five o'clock in the morning.

He realized that they had been sitting there staring at each other in silence for several minutes, which wasn't getting them anywhere.

"All right," he said with a shrug. "I'll go first. My name is Greg Duncan. I'm a friend of Tim's from Missouri. Tim and I have been friends for more years than I can remember. He lets me use this place whenever it's available." He paused and, with a slight lift of his brow, added, "Obviously it wasn't as available as I thought. Now then, who are you?"

Brandi had had an opportunity to calm down a little. Her heart had finally slowed enough that she was fairly certain it wasn't going to leave her chest or go into cardiac arrest.

"I'm Brandi Martin."

As though they were meeting at a formal party, Greg nodded his head slightly and held out his hand. "How do you do, Brandi Martin?"

She stared at his hand blankly, feeling more than a little confused at the sudden polite turn to the conversation. When he continued to hold it out to her, she reluctantly placed her hand in his.

Greg smiled as she immediately withdrew her hand from his. "Rest assured that I have no intention of harming you in any way," he said in a quiet tone. "I apologize for startling you earlier, but quite frankly I had no idea you were in this bed with me."

"I had no idea you were here, either," she replied faintly.

"Yes, you did manage to convince me of that," he said solemnly. "I take it you're a friend of Tim's."

She nodded.

"Would you like to tell me what you're doing here?"

"Trying to sleep," she pointed out dryly.

He laughed. "Good point. Are you here to meet Tim? Are you expecting him soon?"

Greg noted that she appeared to be ill at ease with his questions, but he refused to withdraw them. He just waited patiently, knowing that most people were unnerved by silence, particularly when it came after a question directed toward them.

She dropped her gaze to the colorful quilt that covered the bed. "I was looking for Tim. I thought he might be here."

"Well, as you can see, he isn't."

Her eyes flashed as she met his inquiring gaze. "I know that now. But it was too late when I got here to go back, and I really didn't know where to go. I knew that Tim wouldn't mind— He once showed me where he kept an extra key, and I needed to—" She dropped her eyes and stared at her hands for a moment before continuing, "I needed a place to stay."

"So Tim doesn't know you're here; is that right?"

She shook her head, her gaze still on her hands folded in her lap.

"Where do you live, Brandi?"

"In northern Colorado."

That was vague enough, Greg decided. He decided to try a different tack. "Why did you need to find a place to stay?"

She met his intent gaze and knew that she couldn't tell him about the bizarre happenings of the past few days. Even if he believed her, telling him wouldn't change the danger she was running from.

When she let the silence grow, he sighed. "How old are you, Brandi?"

Startled by the personal question, she asked, "What difference does my age make?"

"It could make a great deal of difference," he said gently, "if you've run away from home and your family is worried about you."

The choked laugh she gave showed no sign of amusement. "I don't know who you are, Mr. Duncan, but you certainly aren't a very good judge of women's ages. How old do you think I am?"

She raised her chin and stared at him almost belligerently, and it was all he could do not to smile. He guessed she was sixteen—maybe—but he could tell that to suggest such a tender age would only incense her. So he chose blatant flattery. "Twenty?"

For the first time since he'd turned on the light, Greg saw honest amusement in her face. She glanced at him, then at the soft glow from the bedside lamp.

"Remind me to always stay in dimly lighted rooms. The light just took several years off my age."

Greg gave a start. Surely she must be lying. But why? And at the moment he had other, more important considerations to face, like trying to get caught up on some much-needed sleep.

"Look, I'm sorry, but I've been up for almost twenty-four hours and I'm dead on my feet. If it's all right with you, I'd like to postpone this meeting until sometime later in the morning."

He waited for a response. When she continued to watch him without saying anything, he shook his head. The chill of the room was making itself felt. With sudden decisiveness he stood and shucked off his pants, then yanked the covers up and crawled beneath them. He was still almost a foot away from her.

Glancing over his shoulder, he added, "Just do me a favor, okay? Try not to scream if I accidentally brush against you again. I promise to do my best to stay on my own side of the bed."

With that he turned off the light and pulled the covers over his broad shoulders, his back to her.

Brandi sat there stunned for a moment, startled by his attitude.

"But you can't sleep here—"

Without moving, he muttered, "Watch me."

"But I don't know you! I mean, you could be—"

"I'll sign an oath in blood not to touch your body if you'll just shut up and let me get some sleep now. We can spend all day tomorrow talking, okay?"

Brandi continued to sit there staring at his back with dismay mixed with a certain amount of admiration. Here was a man who could handle himself in an unusual situation. Her unexplained presence hadn't fazed him.

Brandi slowly slid back down into the bed, making sure the distance between them did not lessen. What was she going to do? Obviously, her options were

limited. She could get up, get dressed and start hiking
down the side of the mountain.

And then what? She could call . . . who? Who could
she call if she couldn't find Tim? Who could she trust?
Who would believe her bizarre story, anyway? She had
no way of knowing why she was being pursued with
such single-minded zest.

If only she weren't so tired, perhaps she could think
straighter. Brandi knew that her behavior bordered on
paranoia, but how could she help it? In her case, there
really seemed to be an Indian behind every tree. And
she didn't know what guise he would be wearing.

At least she felt safer here at Tim's. Surely no one
had been able to follow her here.

She turned and stared at the blond head that seemed
to be buried in the pillow next to her. For now she
might as well follow his example and get some sleep.
Maybe everything would look better tomorrow. She
didn't know Greg Duncan or what he did, but he was
quick-witted enough to make her feel like a witness
being cross-examined. Perhaps she would tell him
what had happened to her tomorrow, when the sun
was shining and everything looked brighter.

Brandi slipped into sleep once again, unaware of
how she was drawn to the body heat nearby, unaware
of curling up to a broad back and feeling safe for the
first time in days.

Greg came awake instantly when he felt Brandi press
closely against his back. He waited for her to say
something, and when she didn't he realized that she
was sound asleep. He smiled to himself without moving and drifted off to sleep once more.

The alluring aroma of freshly brewed coffee drifted into Brandi's dreams several hours later. Without opening her eyes, she stretched luxuriously, feeling rested, relaxed and more like her old self than she had in days.

When she awakened enough to register the smell, her eyes blinked open and she stared at the slanted roof over her head.

She wasn't at home, because there was no one there to prepare coffee and the ceiling of her bedroom was not formed by two of the bedroom walls coming together to meet overhead.

It was only then that she remembered the night before, and glanced at the other side of the bed. She had a certain sense of a good-news-bad-news situation. The good news was that she was alone. The bad news was that she was not on her side of the bed, or even in the middle. To be technically accurate, Brandi had awakened on the same side of the bed that had been occupied by Greg Duncan. She could only hope that she had moved restlessly after he had gotten up. Otherwise, she knew that she wouldn't be able to face him without her embarrassment showing.

Now that she was awake, she became aware of other sounds and scents drifting up from downstairs. The mouth-watering aroma of bacon wafted up to greet her, as well as the soft, homey sounds of someone working in the kitchen.

She also caught a distinct hum, as though whoever was in the kitchen were quite pleased with the world. Brandi lunged out of bed, quivering. Had she done something last night to put him in such a benign, even benevolent, mood?

She couldn't remember. She shook her head, then realized that it was too cold to stand there shivering beside the bed trying to remember what she might have done last night. She found her clothes where she had dropped them the night before and hastily pulled on her turtleneck undershirt, a bulky sweater, a long pair of thermal underpants and her jeans. Then she grabbed a pair of thick socks and pulled them on. Her fleece-lined leather boots followed.

Only then did she realize that she had to go to the bathroom, which was downstairs. But at least she felt protected now—against the cold and against the man waiting below.

Greg Duncan from Missouri. If she hadn't been so tired the night before she might have responded differently to his presence. However, once she had accepted that he was a friend of Tim's, she had relaxed, feeling safe—safe for the first time in days. The sleep that overcame her had been like a powerful narcotic, deadening her to everything else.

She grabbed the small zippered bag that contained the few toiletries she had hastily purchased the afternoon before and tiptoed down the stairs, hoping to avoid a confrontation until she was better prepared to meet the day.

"Good morning."

She'd just reached the bottom step of the stairway, and she knew that her luck had run out. Slowly turning toward the kitchen, Brandi smiled tentatively at the man who was leaning casually against the kitchen counter with his ankles crossed, his hands wrapped around a giant mug that contained enticing, steamy coffee.

Seen in the daylight, Greg Duncan was older than she had first guessed. He looked to be in his early forties, the dusting of silver in the blond hair showing only in the bright light. His eyes looked silver, glinting brightly as he studied her.

Brandi had to admit that he was very impressive, not only in his physical build but in the sense of alert intelligence that he seemed to radiate.

"Good morning," she replied in a voice that sounded disgustingly weak.

Greg studied the woman who hovered at the bottom of the stairs watching him with those unforgettable eyes. Now he could see the maturity in her figure and in her face that had been obscured the night before.

He could also see the wariness in her expression, and he felt that he understood it. He had a similar feeling hovering within him. If anyone had told him that he would find himself in bed with a strange young woman within hours of arriving at Tim's place, he would have blasted them all the way into the next county.

After ending his engagement a few years ago, Greg had faced the fact that he was not marriage material. Other than a few casual friendships, he rarely spent any time with women. His work was his life, and he was content with that life.

His vacation was an opportunity to spend a few days away from his career and relax. It was not a time to be entertaining a curly-headed waif with large sapphire-blue eyes, and especially not one who looked at him as though he might attack her at any moment.

He smiled at the thought of her curling up to his back earlier. Did she remember that? He couldn't forget waking up this morning to find her head resting on his shoulder and his arm wrapped securely around her, holding her close to his side. His leg had been securely held down by her thigh, which had rested across him. Her fingers had rested trustingly on his chest, as though she were reassured by the steady rhythm of his heart beating beneath her palm.

Being the normal, healthy male that he was, Greg had had an immediate physical reaction to the provocative situation, and he had had to decide what to do about it. Despite his body's eager suggestions, Greg's mind had won the day.

Greg's mind took control of every situation in which he found himself, regardless of what he might be feeling.

So, although he had clearly registered how appealing she looked cuddled so snugly against him, Greg had eased away from her until he'd been out of bed. Then he had tucked the covers around her and left her sleeping soundly while he'd dressed.

By the time he'd showered, started a fire in the fireplace and had his coffee poured, Greg had a list of questions that he fully intended to have answered by his unexpected and impromptu roommate.

"Would you like some coffee?" he asked.

Brandi had noticed his smile as he had carefully studied her, and she knew that she must look a mess. Holding up the bag, she pointed to the bathroom. "Yes, as soon as I get presentable."

He nodded and straightened, reaching for another mug.

Greg watched her disappear into the bathroom and close the door, then slowly poured her coffee, wondering what tactic to use to get Brandi Martin to talk.

When she reappeared in the kitchen a few minutes later she had combed her hair and no doubt washed her face, but she was still pale, and he could count the tiny smattering of freckles across the bridge of her nose. She'd made no attempt to hide the slight shadows beneath her eyes.

"How do you like your eggs?" he asked, motioning for her to sit down. He had such an air of authority about him that she responded automatically, sinking onto one of the bench seats by the table.

"Over easy," she replied, vaguely surprised to see him place a skillet over one of the burners. Brandi hadn't realized she was hungry until the smell of the bacon had caused her stomach to growl earlier. She couldn't remember the last time she'd eaten.

Brandi picked up the cup he'd placed on the table and took a swallow of the revitalizing liquid. Her eyes were drawn back to the man before her. He made everything he did appear to be easy. There were no wasted moves, no unnecessary searching for things. Everything had been laid out as though waiting for her to appear. He tapped an egg on the side of the pan, breaking it open with one hand and gently letting it slide into the pan.

"Are you a professional cook?" she found herself asking.

Greg glanced around, then back to what he was doing. "I'm a professional eater. I discovered a long time ago that if I didn't feed myself there was a strong possibility I'd starve."

"Oh." She continued to watch him for a few minutes in silence, then was appalled to hear herself ask, "Are you married?"

He laughed. "No. Why do you ask?"

She could feel herself blushing. "No reason."

"Are you?"

"Married?"

"That was the topic under discussion, I believe."

"No. No, I'm not."

"Then you aren't running away from a husband, either."

"What makes you keep thinking that I'm running away? I just needed a place to stay for a few days, that's all."

He slipped two eggs onto a warmed plate, put freshly buttered toast and crisp bacon beside it and set the dish in front of her. She stared at it until he said, "Eat before it gets cold." Picking up her cup, he refilled it and handed it back to her. Then he quickly prepared his plate and sat down across from her.

"Why were you looking for Tim?" he asked, ignoring her last question.

"What are you, a reporter?"

"No. I'm a lawyer. So why don't you answer my question?"

"Because it's none of your business."

"That's true. However, something seems to be bothering you, and if I knew what it was, perhaps I could help."

"Well, at least that explains your cross-examination style of conversation," she said, finishing the last bite of food on her plate and relaxing back in her seat with a sigh. She picked up her cup and sipped. "You serve a mean breakfast, Mr. Duncan. Thank you. I hadn't realized how hungry I was."

"You're welcome. I must say that you have a real knack for sidestepping my questions."

She grinned. "Being around Tim taught me how to do that, although I was never very successful at keeping things from him."

"How long have you known Tim?"

She shrugged. "All my life."

"Are you a relative of his?" he asked, knowing full well that Tim was an only child. But she might be a cousin.

"Not by blood, no. But in every way possible, Tim has been like a big brother to me. He's always been there when I needed him." Almost under her breath, she added, "and, boy, do I need him now."

Greg got up and refilled their cups, then sat down again. "Have you talked to him recently?"

She shook her head. "I tried calling his apartment, but all I could get was his recording machine. I left messages, but there's no way of knowing when he'll get them. I also tried another number he once gave me in case of an emergency, but that didn't get me anywhere."

"What do you mean?"

"Oh, I got some sort of answering service. They said they never heard of a Tim Walker. I must have gotten the number wrong or something."

"So you came here, hoping to find him."

"Yes."

"How did you get here?"

She was quiet for several minutes before she answered in a quiet voice. "I took a bus from Denver, then had a taxi bring me up here."

"A taxi! We're at least twenty miles out of town."

"I know."

"Don't you think you could tell me what's going on?" he asked. Not only was his curiosity stirred, but he was surprised to discover a feeling of compassion for this woman, who was obviously on edge.

Brandi replaced her cup on the table with a slight thump and stared at the insistent man across from her. "I'm trying to get away from some men who are trying to kill me."

Chapter Two

Greg recognized the distraught expression on Brandi's face. More than one client had come to him for help wearing a similar expression. He also recognized that she needed to talk. Speaking in a soothing tone, he slowly stood and said, "Why don't we take our coffee and sit in front of that gorgeous fire in there? We might as well enjoy it while we talk, don't you think?"

He picked up both cups and led the way, confident that she would follow him. He placed her cup on the end table by the long, comfortable sofa facing the fireplace. Then he gracefully folded his long legs and sank onto the rug.

Brandi felt as though she no longer had a will of her own. After a good night's sleep and a decent meal, she was beginning to feel as though she'd just awakened from a nightmare and that none of the strange happenings of the past few days were real. Only the man waiting so patiently for her in front of the fireplace seemed to have any meaning at the moment.

He wanted her to tell him why she was there. At this point, she hardly knew herself. She had been running away, but she wasn't sure from what. She had been looking for Tim, but she wasn't sure why.

"Ahhh," he said, watching her as she slowly followed him into the room. "This is my idea of living. No phones ringing, no demands being made on my time. Just a warm fire—" he waved toward the scene on the other side of the glass, "—a picture-perfect scene outside, and someone to talk with."

Brandi sat down on the sofa and picked up her cup as though it were the only security she had to cling to at the moment.

"What happened, Brandi, that has frightened you so?" he asked, his voice soft and gentle. It seemed to flow over and around her, soothing her somehow.

"I live in a rural area, in the foothills," she began, staring down at the coffee in her cup. "I live alone, but it has never bothered me before, living alone. I like the quiet, the solitude, the opportunity to work long, uninterrupted hours."

"What do you do?"

Her eyes slowly lifted until they met his. "I make inlaid designs in wood—marquetry. Jewelry boxes, tabletops, room dividers, whatever I think might sell."

"Sounds interesting."

"I enjoy it. I spend a lot of time outdoors, looking for some of nature's designs that I can duplicate—" she glanced out the window and nodded "—such as that limb that is almost touching the deck railing."

Greg glanced where she indicated and saw a branch weighted down with snow. Pine cones hung in a cluster at the end. He had never really noticed the symmetry of such an arrangement before.

"You must have a special eye for beauty," he admitted with a smile.

"I love nature. I enjoy each season, and I spend a great deal of my time exploring, snapping pictures, looking for ideas."

"You seem very content with your choice of a life."

"I am. At least I was, until I realized how vulnerable I am. I don't have any close neighbors." She turned her head until she was facing him once more. "I prefer to be independent."

Greg had so many questions, but he was hesitant to break into her story. Now that she was slowly opening up, he didn't want to distract her with interruptions.

She paused, as though thinking about what she wanted to say next. "We had snow last week, and that left everything so beautifully fresh and bright. I decided to take my cross-country skis up into the hills and explore. I've had plenty of time since then to regret the impulse."

"What happened?"

"I'm not sure exactly where I was in the hills. I know that there are some military installations up there, but I'm positive that I didn't accidentally go into a restricted area. After all, they're carefully marked." She took a quick sip of her coffee. "I was high up on the side of a hill, and as I rounded a crest, something below was detonated. I looked down and saw some sort of rough encampment. Men dressed in white and

carrying some type of hand weapons were watching as
something—I don't know how to describe it—began
to climb into the sky, higher and higher. I stood there
and stared. I didn't know what to think. Then I heard
shouts, and when I glanced back down I saw men
pointing at me and yelling. I started to wave back
when I realized that they were angry, running in my
direction and aiming their weapons at me!"

"What did you do?"

"I managed to turn and ski away as quickly as possible. Luckily, I had a long downhill slope ahead of
me, and I was able to reach the shelter of trees before
they spotted me." She shivered at the memory. "They
began to fire into the trees."

Greg leaned forward. "They actually shot at you?"

She nodded.

"What did you do?"

"I kept going as fast as I could. I think the only
thing that saved me was that my four-wheel-drive
Blazer wasn't all that far away. I managed to get to the
car, removed my skis and left."

"Did you see the men again?"

"Not right away, no. I really thought I'd managed
to lose them. Then, several miles down the road, I
happened to glance up and saw something following
me."

"What was it?"

"I don't know. It was too big for a car. It looked
like a camouflaged truck of some sort. You know the
kind you see in army movies—big, with a heavy grill
in front."

"What did you do?"

"I realized that I couldn't go home. I would really be isolated then. I didn't even slow down at the road where I live. Instead, I kept driving."

"Did they continue to follow you?"

"Yes. I was lucky to get into fairly busy traffic and managed to gain some distance on them. I was afraid to stop until I made it into town."

"You got to town, then?"

"Yes. I decided to go to the sheriff's office and report what I saw. I hid the Blazer on a back street and walked to the sheriff's office. Only when I got there—" She stopped and swallowed hard.

"When you got there—" he prompted.

"I had just turned the corner to the sheriff's office when I saw his door open and he came out—talking with two men dressed in white, wearing some kind of white military hats!"

"Did you recognize the men?"

"No. Only the way they were dressed. They wore the same type of clothing as the men I'd seen in the hills."

"What did you do?"

"I dodged back around the corner and waited. I could hear them talking and laughing. I heard the sheriff say he'd run a check on the license number right away and get back to them."

"Do you think they were talking about you?"

"I have no idea, but I was too scared to take a chance." She took a hasty sip of coffee. "That's when I decided to call Tim."

"Why Tim?"

"Because I know he's got some kind of connection with the government and I thought he might know what was going on."

"But he wasn't there."

"No. I filled the Blazer with gas and decided to drive to Denver, hoping to get lost in the larger city. After I got there, I knew I needed to hide the Blazer and get out of my ski clothes. So I parked in a parking garage and went to a local department store and bought these." She looked down at her sweater and pants. "I tried a couple more times to reach Tim, then decided to look for him here." She ran her hand through her short curls. "I was afraid to use the Blazer, so I came by bus."

Brandi took a deep breath, then slowly exhaled. Somehow, talking about it had helped. She was no closer to finding a solution, but sharing what she had gone through with another person had eased the tight band that seemed to have constricted her chest for days.

They sat before the fire in companionable silence for several minutes.

Greg recognized that Brandi believed she was being pursued. He was certain that what she had experienced had been very traumatic. It wasn't surprising that she had reacted so violently. However, he also knew that she could easily have misunderstood what she had seen and heard.

But he couldn't be sure. There was always the slim possibility that she might be in danger. That possibility gave him pause. Tim wasn't here. They didn't know when he'd return, but Greg knew him well enough to know he would respond as soon as he heard Brandi's messages.

"Did you tell Tim you were coming here?"

"Yes."

"Good," he said with some satisfaction. "Then I think you'd better wait until he shows up."

"Which could be in a day, a week, a month—or next summer sometime," she pointed out.

"Well, let's give it some time, okay? If he hasn't shown up in a few days, then I'll take you back home and see what we can find out, okay?"

She looked at him in surprise. "You'd do that for me?"

"Sure. Why not?"

"You don't know me."

"Any little sister of Tim's is a sister of mine," he said with a grin. "Of course, I was rather hoping to get some skiing in first. So if you don't mind waiting here a few days—" He paused, looking at her expectantly.

"I don't mind," she responded slowly. She looked around the room. "I can always sleep down here."

"I'm sure we can work out something." Greg got to his feet. "Now, then. Why don't we run into town and get you some ski equipment." He glanced at what she was wearing. "Did you bring your ski clothes?"

She nodded. "I have them in a bag upstairs, with another change of clothes."

"Great. Then let's run to town and find you some skis."

"You don't think they followed me?"

He allowed himself to smile slightly. "I think you were very clever eluding them. If anything, they are probably watching either your house or your car at the parking garage."

She stood up with a pleased smile. "You really think so?"

He nodded. "Yes. I'm impressed with your quick thinking."

"Then you don't think I overreacted?"

"I think you were playing it safe. I also think Tim will agree with me." He held out his hand. "Come on, let's go."

Hours later, Greg and Brandi were a fair distance from the cabin. Greg had quickly discovered that Brandi was quite adept at getting around on skis. She seemed to be enjoying herself, and he was hard-pressed to keep up with her.

During the past several hours, he'd gotten a glimpse of another side of her personality. She was quick to smile, and he discovered that he enjoyed provoking her smile. Although shadows sometimes lurked in the depths of her beautiful eyes, she seemed to be making an effort to relax.

He paused, looking around. Her bright red ski jacket should have been easy to spot, but at the moment he could see nothing but the snowy expanse around him, the dark brown and dull green of the pine trees.

"Brandi? Slow down, okay? I'm not in quite as good shape as I thought I was," he said.

Everything was quiet. She didn't answer. Greg had a slight sense of unease. He began to follow her tracks over the side of the hill.

A sudden avalanche of snow fell on his head and shoulders, and he yelped. The limb he'd paused under had just been shaken clear of its weight of snow. Greg heard delighted laughter behind him, and turned and saw Brandi peeking around the tree.

He slipped out of his skis and made a lunge for her, bringing her to the ground. Her squeal echoed in the clear air.

"That was unfair and uncalled-for," he said, pushing her so that she lost her balance and fell back into a snowbank. Greg began to laugh at her outraged expression. Every time she tried to get up, she lost her balance and fell back. Finally he walked over and offered her his hand, only to find himself jerked off balance. He fell face first into the snow beside her.

He came up sputtering, grabbed a handful of snow and mashed it into her face.

The afternoon's skiing was soon reduced to a snow fight deluxe.

Eventually Greg managed to subdue his opponent by the simple expedient of sitting on her and pinning both arms out away from her body with his hands.

"Do you give up?"

"Never! I never give up!" she managed to yell breathlessly.

"Even when you can't even move?" he asked, laughing.

"I can move! I can—" She kicked out with both legs but couldn't hit him. "Get off me, you big oaf! I can't breathe! Tim would never have—"

"I know. Tim, no doubt, always lets you win. That's why you're so spoiled."

"Spoiled! I'm not spoiled. I just—"

"You're just used to getting your own way, that's obvious." He grinned down at her. "Now, then. Do you give up?"

Brandi lay in the snow and looked up at the big man above her. He'd lost his cap in the tussle, and his blond hair fell rather endearingly across his forehead. His cheeks were red from exertion and he was wet, but for the first time Brandi saw a part of him that she hadn't guessed existed—a playful part. He looked years younger as he watched her warily, his smile gleaming brightly. His eyes, which had seemed so cold to her earlier, now sparkled with silver glints, and there were dancing imps in their depths.

Why, he's gorgeous! she suddenly realized. Gone was the implacable, pragmatic lawyer she had spent the day with. Here was a man who radiated a warmth and virility that caused her heart to set up an increased drumming in her chest.

She stared up at him, entranced by what she saw. Perhaps her expression gave her away, because Brandi noticed that Greg's smile slowly altered and the warmth in his eyes seemed to increase. He shifted so that his weight was no longer on her, but she didn't move. Not even when he lowered his head toward hers and placed his mouth on hers.

His lips felt warm as they tentatively touched hers. Brandi's eyes drifted closed, and she shyly returned his kiss.

Greg pulled her into his arms, holding her against his chest while he continued to explore the soft contours of her mouth. By the time he pulled away slightly, they were both warm and flushed.

Brandi didn't know what to say. She felt as though she had practically melted into his arms. She couldn't remember the last time she'd been so affected by a kiss. And this one had come from a man she hardly knew. *And you've agreed to stay with him,* she reminded herself. *What is he going to think about you now?*

Greg got to his feet and pulled her up beside him. He began to dust himself off without looking at her. "We'd better get back. It will be dark soon."

"Yes" was all she could think of to say.

They found their skis and put them on again. Then Greg took the lead and they followed their tracks back to the cabin.

Greg couldn't believe what he had done. He'd wanted Brandi to feel comfortable about staying there for a few days in case Tim showed up, but then he'd ruined it by doing something stupid like kiss her.

There was no telling what she was thinking at the moment. She was without transportation, totally at his mercy. The last thing he wanted her to think was that he would take advantage of the situation.

And yet that was just what he had done. And why?

He couldn't really explain his reaction to Brandi. She was young, too young for him. They were totally different in temperament. Now that she was no longer frightened, Greg could see that Brandi was normally friendly and outgoing. He, on the other hand, had trouble relating to people. He was good at what he did professionally, but he was a failure at relationships.

But he couldn't deny his attraction to Brandi. Perhaps it was because of her warm and friendly personality. He didn't know. All that he knew for sure was that he felt the same way around her as he felt after he'd built a brightly burning fire—as though he could warm himself and find comfort near that flame.

Somehow Brandi had become a flame to him. He had to be careful that he didn't singe himself.

By the time they reached the cabin, dark shadows surrounded the area. They had come around the side of the house so that they could enter through the kitchen door when Greg abruptly paused.

Brandi almost ran into him. She stopped and began to unfasten her skis.

"Stay here," he said in a low voice.

She glanced up, disturbed by the strange note in his voice. "What's wrong?"

He motioned for her to be quiet and stepped out of his skis. Stealthily he moved closer to the cabin, silently signaling that she should stay where she was.

Greg disappeared around the corner, only to reappear in a few minutes, motioning her to join him.

"What's wrong?"

"We had some company while we were gone." He pointed to two pairs of tracks leading up the driveway to the house.

"Maybe it was the people who check on the place for Tim."

"Maybe."

"Did they go inside?"

"If they did, nothing was disturbed. They aren't in there now. I checked."

When they got inside, Brandi shivered. She was feeling the effects of their snow fight.

"Why don't you get your shower while I build up the fire again?" he suggested.

She glanced around and saw the solemn stranger she had seen earlier in the day. Gone was the laughing, loving man who had kissed her earlier. Brandi discovered that she missed that man. She had a hunch that very few had ever seen him.

"All right. Then I'll find us something for dinner while you change."

Greg watched Brandi go into the bathroom and shut the door. Then he went over to the fireplace and began to blow on the coals. As soon as the new logs were burning, he straightened and looked around the room. As far as he could tell, nothing had been disturbed. The intruders had been professionals. He didn't like that, not at all. Having someone break in while they were gone gave more credence to Brandi's story.

Of course, he was going to let Brandi believe it was the couple who kept an eye on the place. There was no reason to make her more nervous. She was just now beginning to relax for the first time in days.

He was glad she hadn't looked at the door. Whoever had gotten in had not had a key, but they had managed to enter easily enough. Professionals.

Now Greg knew for certain that he couldn't leave Brandi until this whole mess was resolved. He just hoped that Tim got in touch soon. Brandi had been right. Tim had the contacts.

In the meantime, Greg had to make sure that Brandi was kept safe—from whoever was hunting her, and from himself.

Chapter Three

Dinner was over, and once again Brandi found herself sitting in front of the fireplace, alternately watching the flames and the man who sat on the rug nearby staring into the fire as though learning the secrets of the universe.

He'd been quiet during dinner, although he had complimented her on her imaginative casserole. However, Brandi had felt his distraction and wondered about it.

Was he thinking about the kiss they had shared earlier? She had found it a little disturbing herself, partly because the action seemed to be so out of character for this man. But then, she recognized that she really didn't know much about him. And she was discovering that she wanted to learn a great deal more about him.

"Greg—" she began, just as he turned.

"Brandi—" he murmured simultaneously.

They both smiled and said, "Go ahead." They began to laugh.

"What were you going to say?" she asked.

"I was just going to ask you about Tim. How you met, that sort of thing."

"Oh. Well, that's easy enough. We grew up next door to each other." She wondered why he seemed to withdraw a little at her words. "I was eight when my father died. Mom and I were taken care of financially, but I'm afraid we were both rather helpless. Tim's family adopted us, looking after things, seeing that repairs were made, inviting us to family gatherings, that sort of thing."

He nodded, as though waiting for her to continue.

"That's about it. Mom died in my second year of college. She'd appointed Tim the trustee of my financial estate." She laughed. "He's only a few years older than I am, but he's always been so responsible. She knew he would look after me, and he has."

"I'm surprised you haven't married him," he offered, looking into the flames rather than at her.

"Marry Tim?" she repeated, surprised at the idea. "It would have been like marrying my brother. I mean, we don't see each other in that light. Tim has always been there for me—" she paused, thinking about the past few days "—well, almost always, but he's not the least bit interested in me romantically, I assure you."

"I suppose I'm just surprised that someone like you is not already married," he said finally.

"Someone like me? What does that mean?"

"You have so much to offer a man."

"I do? I would hardly agree with that. I get too wrapped up in my work to pay attention to what is going on around me."

"You're a great cook."

"Thank you, kind sir. But then, I forced myself to concentrate. Besides, casseroles are easy—you dump the ingredients together, stick it in the oven and wait for the timer to go off." She grinned. "Of course, there have been times when I was concentrating so much on my work that I didn't hear the timer. The first thing I knew, the smoke alarm alerted me that dinner was slightly overdone."

They laughed at the verbal picture she painted.

"How about you? Why aren't you married?" she said after a few moments.

"I almost was, once."

She waited, but he didn't say anything more. "Don't tell me you're going to stop there, leaving my curiosity unrelieved?"

"It's a very boring story, really," he offered reluctantly.

"Nonsense. I can't believe you'd be involved in a romance that was boring." Her adamant remark surprised them both, and she found herself blushing.

Greg watched her discomfort with amusement. He was a little surprised by her comment. He knew himself very well and recognized that he was in fact more than a little boring. His surprise was that she hadn't already seen that.

Greg had never talked about his engagement to Penny Blackwell to anyone. It was a closed chapter in his life. Now, for some reason, he found himself wanting to look at it again, with another person. To be more precise, he wanted to share what had happened with Brandi Martin. More surprises.

He stood up and walked over to the small cabinet where Tim kept his liquor. Picking up a bottle, he said, "How about a snifter of brandy while I tell my tale of unrequited love?"

She wrinkled her nose. "Despite the name, I've never cared for the taste of the stuff. Does Tim stock any amaretto?"

He found the appropriate bottle and poured her a glass, then joined her in front of the fire once more. This time he sat down on the sofa beside her, handing her one of the glasses he held in his hands.

"I had a large law practise in St. Louis and decided to move to Payton, a small town that reminded me of the hometown where I'd grown up back east. Penny Blackwell taught high school in Payton. We were introduced. I noticed that she didn't seem to be dating anyone, so I began to ask her out. The more I was with her, the more I came to love her. After we'd dated for several months, I asked her to marry me. She accepted."

Greg had started off in a matter-of-fact tone of voice, as though he were explaining the facts of a case to a jury. However, Brandi heard a hesitancy toward the end, as though a slight note of pain had colored the timbre of his voice, when he'd mentioned his proposal and her acceptance.

For the first time, Brandi recognized that this strong, self-assured, almost arrogant man also had a vulnerability to him that was almost as appealing to her as the lightheartedness that had peeked out at her earlier in the day—just before he'd shared a kiss with her. She was fairly sure that few people had seen this side of him, either.

Now that he was talking, Greg discovered that it wasn't going to be as easy to relive the past as he had first thought. He took a sip of his drink and wondered how he could change the subject without being too obvious.

"What happened?" Brandi asked softly. Greg heard compassion and caring in her voice. He was touched. She didn't know him very well, and yet she recognized that what he was telling her was difficult.

"Well..." he said, pausing to clear his throat. "What I never realized during that time was that there was another man in her life—a man she'd grown up with who lived next door to her." He glanced over at Brandi. "Rather like you and Tim, from what you tell me." His gaze returned to the fire. "Only, in Penny's case, Brad had moved away and become a well-known television actor." He took a sip of his drink. "Have you ever heard of Brad Crawford?"

"Brad Crawford? You mean the hunk on *Hope for Tomorrow*?" she asked in surprise.

"That's Brad, all right. I found out a week before our wedding that Brad was Penny's childhood sweetheart."

"Then there's no parallel between Tim and me, that's for sure," she said with a chuckle. "What happened? Did Penny call off the wedding?"

"No."

She watched him for a moment in silence. "I'm afraid I don't understand."

"Neither did I, at first. It took me a few days to recognize the fact that Penny really did think she loved me and that she wanted to marry me. She didn't seem to realize how bonded she and Brad truly were. After spending hours analyzing the situation, I finally had to face the fact that what Penny wanted from me was the settled, comfortable, nonthreatening existence that I could provide for her.''

"She was actually going to marry you, even though she was in love with someone else?''

"I don't think she understood her feelings toward Brad at the time. There was a lot of resentment and anger on her part. And yet—'' he paused and absently ran his hand through his hair, mussing it in a way that Brandi found peculiarly attractive in this carefully ordered man ''—it's tough to explain, but Penny came alive whenever Brad was around. She sparkled and glowed. He seemed to bring out all of her emotions, so that she practically vibrated with energy whenever he was around her.''

He stood up and put another log on the fire. "Penny taught me so much. I had never felt so much love toward another person, not since I was a child. She brought my feelings to the surface, and I'll admit I was uncomfortable having to face them. But because she had taught me what love was all about, I recognized what was happening. I wasn't the man she needed to make her life complete. She was settling for less because she was afraid to reach out and grab what life was truly offering her.''

"That must have been a very painful conclusion for you to come to.''

He was surprised that she saw that so quickly. He nodded, unable for the moment to find the words to agree.

"You loved her. You loved her enough to understand that your loving her wasn't right for her. You loved her enough to let her go."

"I don't think I looked at it quite so unselfishly, I'm afraid. If I'd thought our relationship had a chance of working out, I'm sure I would have fought for what we had. But I knew it was only a question of time before Penny recognized what she had given up by not marrying Brad. I didn't want to stay around and watch her gradual disillusionment."

"So what happened? Did *you* call off the wedding?"

"I'm afraid I wasn't that honorable about it. I just didn't show up."

Brandi set her glass down abruptly and stared at Greg in shocked dismay. "What? You mean you let Penny show up at the church without telling her you'd changed your mind? How horrible!"

"Yes, Brad expressed similar sentiments to me the day before the wedding when I told him of my intentions."

She stared at the man sitting beside her, unable to comprehend anyone behaving in such a cold and callous manner. "Poor Penny."

"I was hoping you would give me a little credit for understanding human nature better than to think that Brad would allow her to be humiliated in front of everyone. By telling him my intentions ahead of time, I knew that I was giving him an opportunity to save the day. I deliberately made myself look like a heel. Otherwise, I was fairly sure that Penny would insist on going through with the marriage and ignoring how she felt toward Brad."

"But still—"

"I know. What I did was cowardly and reprehensible."

"And if you had it to do over again, you'd do it the same way."

"Yes."

"Because you didn't think you could face Penny and tell her."

"What makes you say that?"

"It was easier for you to play the cold-blooded reptile for Brad than to admit to Penny that you loved her enough to let her go."

"Now you're trying to make me a martyr. I'm far from that."

"And you're still in love with Penny."

"Of course not."

"How long ago did this happen?"

"Four or five years ago. Why?"

"And you've still not married?"

He laughed. "Not because I've been nursing a broken heart, I assure you. I enjoy my life the way it is. Instead of relinquishing my practice in St. Louis, I've managed to keep both offices open and busy. I don't have time for a personal life. Nor, to be honest, do I find the idea particularly appealing."

"Because you're afraid of being hurt."

"Now you're trying to romanticize me. Penny would have become bored with me very quickly. She quit teaching and moved to New York with Brad right after they married. As a matter of fact, they starred together in a Broadway play last spring."

"Oh, I remember that now. The character Brad plays—what's his name? Drew Derek?—disappeared and was missing for several months."

"I wouldn't know. I never watch the daily serials."

Brandi tilted her head and studied him. "So you were once engaged to marry Brad Crawford's wife."

"My one claim to fame."

She continued to study him. "You know, there's a definite resemblance between the two of you, now that you mention it."

"I didn't."

"Except that you don't smile as much."

"The courtroom doesn't encourage the practice."

"But you're as good at acting as he is."

He looked at her, startled by her comment. "But I'm not an actor."

"You've been putting on quite a performance right now, trying to convince me that your engagement and the ending of it hasn't had a profound effect on who you are and what you've become."

"Are you part witch or something?"

She laughed. "No, of course not. If I were, I would have conjured up a spell to have those men who are chasing me turned into tadpoles or something."

"And you could also figure out where Tim is at the moment."

She laughed. "I gave up trying to keep up with Tim years ago."

"A wise decision," he said quietly.

Brandi leaned forward, gazing into Greg's suddenly serious eyes. "I take it that you know what Tim does for a living."

Watching her warily, he said, "Maybe."

She shrugged. "I don't want to know. Not really. All I know is that it's dangerous and that he's very good at what he does."

"Yes. And yes."

"That's why I thought of him when I needed help. I think Tim has the contacts to find out what's going on up there in the hills."

"There's a strong possibility you're right."

Brandi stared into her glass, remembering her fright and wondering if she was safe even now. . . .

"Brandi?"

She glanced up. "Hmm?"

He took the empty glass from her hand and set it on the table nearby. "Try to put it out of your mind, okay?"

She nodded. "I'm trying."

"You're safe now. I'm not going to leave you until Tim shows up or we go back to Denver to try to get some answers without him." He recalled the unidentified footprints he'd seen earlier. "I'm not going to allow anyone to harm you."

She believed him. Here was a man who instinctively made her feel sheltered and protected. He might not be willing to share his innermost feelings, but he was willing to share his strength. At the moment, that was enough, but Brandi couldn't help wondering how it would feel to have this strong, polished, arrogant man in love with her. Would he allow her to see more than occasional glimpses of those other personalities hidden deep inside?

Brandi had never had a close relationship with a man in a romantic sense. She'd purposely avoided them because she was afraid. The loss of her father at an early age had been traumatic. Losing her mother while she was still in college hadn't helped her to come to terms with her fear of getting close to someone.

She had needed to learn how to be independent so that she would never be hurt like that again. Tim had understood her need for independence and had given her plenty of room. She'd never fully appreciated his understanding of her until now.

Looking at the man seated beside her, sipping his drink and watching her so intently, she knew that for the first time in years she was in danger of allowing someone to get too close to her. For some reason, she didn't find the thought as threatening as she would have in the past. Perhaps her feelings stemmed from the fact that she had finally met someone who was as shy of becoming involved as she was. Brandi felt as though she were coaxing him out of his protective shell, not the other way around.

"What are you thinking?" he asked, his hand cupping her face in a gentle caress.

"About you," she admitted in a husky voice.

"Very dull."

"Not at all. I was thinking about how little I know about men." She paused, searching for words. "And how much I would like to get to know you better."

"Really?"

"Really."

"That could be dangerous, considering the present situation."

"What do you mean?"

"We're alone in rather isolated circumstances."

She smiled. "I know."

"And you don't feel threatened?"

"Not by you. I feel very safe with you."

"Thank you. I think." He rubbed his thumb softly against her cheek. "I probably represent a father figure to you."

She burst into laughter. "Hardly."

"I feel old enough to be your father."

"I don't see you in that role at all, Greg. I find you very attractive..." She turned her head slightly and kissed his palm, which had been resting along her jawline. "...and very reliable..." She reached up and touched the strand of hair that had fallen across his forehead. "...and very, very sexy..." she whispered, pressing her lips against his.

She felt him tense at her words. Brandi rested her hand lightly against his sweater-covered chest and felt the heavy rhythm of his heart. Despite his lack of expression, he was not unaffected by her. She slid her arms around his neck, pulling him closer.

Greg clearly understood the dangers of this particular situation. A couple in front of a fireplace, relaxed from a large dinner and a glass of liqueur, miles away from any other human beings. They obviously found each other attractive, available and interested. Mother Nature couldn't have planned it better if she had tried.

So it was up to him to keep a grip on reality, to set the tone of the evening, to make sure that nothing happened between them because... because...

Greg's iron will seemed to shatter, and his arms wrapped around Brandi in a strong grip. For the moment, all he could think about was the woman in his arms.

Brandi quickly discovered that the kiss they had shared earlier in the snow had only been a playful sharing. What she was experiencing now was a man's desire for her, something she'd never known before.

Greg held her and kissed her as though he were starved for the taste and touch of her, as though he had waited for centuries to hold her close to him, as though he never intended to let her go.

Brandi reveled in the passionate intensity of the moment. Perhaps this man couldn't talk about his feelings. He might even verbally deny them, but he couldn't hide them completely.

She responded with wholehearted enthusiasm, enjoying the sensation of feeling the surge of power in his heavy shoulder and chest muscles as he held her against him so tightly. Her hands explored the contours of his shoulders and back, wordlessly encouraging him.

Greg pulled away slightly and looked at the small young woman in his arms. Had he lost his mind? What in the hell did he think he was doing? He'd always taken pride in his ability to control himself, and yet...and yet now he seemed to have lost all restraint, all the rational and reasoning processes inside him that he'd come to rely on all these years.

This tiny wisp of a woman seemed to have reduced all his thinking processes to a quivering mass of mush. She lay in his arms with a slight smile on her face, her eyes closed. Her lips were moist and rosy from his earlier possession of them. His mouth unconsciously sought hers once more.

The sudden crackling of the wood in the fireplace several minutes later jerked Greg's thoughts away from Brandi. The loud noise in the otherwise quiet room grabbed his attention. He looked around, forcing himself to regain his self-control.

Brandi was lost to the sensation of the moment. Never in her wildest dreams had she imagined that anyone could affect her in such a way. No wonder so many of her college friends had advocated sexual exploration with their enthusiastic boyfriends.

How could she have possibly missed such a marvelous experience before now?

Greg loosened his hold around her and carefully moved away from what he considered a dangerous and explosive situation. He got up and checked the fire, then walked over and looked out at the moonlit, snow-blanketed night.

"You'd better go on upstairs, Brandi," he said without turning around. "It's late."

"I'm going to sleep down here."

Still without turning around, he said, "No, you're not."

"But the sofa isn't long enough for you."

He finally glanced at her over his shoulder. "I'll be fine. I'll see you in the morning."

"But Greg—"

"Let's not debate the issue, Brandi. I'm afraid I'm not in the mood."

Gone was the passionate man who had held her so closely, kissed her so thoroughly and made her feel as though she were soaring high above the universe. In his place was the arrogant lawyer she had met the night before. Hadn't what they had just shared meant anything to him?

"If you're sure—" she began softly.

"I'm sure."

She walked over to the bottom of the stairs. "I'll get you some blankets and a pillow."

"Thank you."

"Good night, Greg."

"Good night, Brandi."

He waited without turning until he heard her moving overhead. Greg realized that he was shaking. He couldn't believe what had almost happened. He'd lost all control over the situation with a woman who obviously trusted him not to take advantage of their isolation from the rest of the world.

He'd never been affected so strongly by anyone before, not even Penny. How could that be? Penny had taught him everything he knew about loving and caring. So how could he feel such an intense need for Brandi that he was willing to forget all his scruples in his almost uncontrollable desire to make her his.

He'd only meant to hold and comfort her, to reassure her, but as soon as he'd been near her he'd wanted so much more. What a laugh. He, of all people, knew there was nothing more, nothing except disillusionment.

Greg turned and watched Brandi bring blankets and a pillow down the steps. He met her at the bottom of the stairs and took them from her.

"Thanks," he said in a cool tone.

Brandi's bewilderment at his sudden change of mood slowly turned to pain. "You're welcome," she managed to say before turning and slowly walking up the steps again.

What an inscrutable man, she thought. She was surprised by how quickly she'd allowed him to get close to her, both physically and emotionally.

She was determined not to allow it to happen again.

Chapter Four

Several hours later, Greg lay awake on the sofa, watching the trees swaying in the ever-increasing wind. A storm was brewing. He wasn't sure how he felt about that. On the one hand, he knew that anyone watching the cabin would be forced to seek shelter if the weather became severe. On the other hand, he had hoped to scout the area for further signs that the place was in fact under surveillance. Another snowfall would obliterate any clues he might otherwise be able to spot.

He wished to hell he knew how to contact Tim. If he was someplace where he could be contacted, Brandi's innocent call to the agency would be passed on to him. Greg was fairly certain that, despite convincing her that she had a wrong number, whoever had taken her call had managed to get her name. If the relationship between Tim and Brandi was as close as Greg suspected, Tim would waste no time in coming to her rescue.

Greg glanced over at the fire, which was going out. Throwing back the blanket that he'd tossed over himself, he got up, feeling the chill that had already invaded the room. Ignoring the fact that he had stripped down to his underwear, Greg built up the fire once more, making sure it was going before again seeking the comfort of his makeshift bed.

Despite Brandi's protestations, Greg felt certain that there was more than friendship between Tim and Brandi. He could well remember Penny's offhand remarks about Brad. If Tim had watched Brandi grow up, how could he possibly resist her?

Greg punched his pillow and turned over. How ironic that he continued to find himself in situations in which he was odd man out. He had long since recognized his wisdom in removing himself from Penny's life, even though the manner in which he'd done it didn't stand up very well under careful scrutiny.

Despite his love for Penny, he'd been able to distance himself enough from his emotions to make a clear, logical decision based on the facts of the matter.

Why was he having such a difficult time trying to deal with his emotions now?

One of the problems he was having was Brandi herself. He'd never known a woman like her before. She was such a mixture of warmth and impulsiveness, shyness and innocence. He had seen her truly frightened and was impressed by her ability to take care of herself under trying circumstances. He'd found himself eager to hear the peal of her infectious laughter and realized that no one had ever teased and played with him as she had that day in the snow.

Greg couldn't remember the last time he'd played in the snow with anyone, nor could he remember the last time he'd really laughed and enjoyed himself. Somehow, in his pursuit of a career, he'd lost sight of how to enjoy the little things in life.

Brandi had pointed out so many things today while they'd been out exploring: oddly shaped trees, a couple of squirrels, the sudden flash of color from a bird in flight. Even while skiing, he had a tendency to let his mind wander, more often than not trying to solve some knotty legal problem.

Brandi had shown him the fun of being fully conscious of the present. The first time he'd kissed her had been an impulse born out of the joy of sharing that moment with her. Her response had unnerved him, causing him to loosen his control for a few very precious moments.

The more he was around her, the more fascinating Greg found Brandi. He wasn't sure what he was going to do if his hunch was correct and there was more to Tim and Brandi's relationship than she was telling. He respected Tim more than he respected any other human being he knew. If Tim loved and wanted Brandi, Greg had to accept that. In the meantime, he had to get a firm grip on his emotions and not let them overpower him.

The situation at the moment was tense enough without his having to battle his sudden and totally unexplainable reaction to Brandi.

Turning onto his side, Greg determinedly closed his eyes. He had to get some sleep.

* * *

Brandi saw the men coming after her and tried to turn and get away, but one of her skis wouldn't move. She tugged and tugged, frantic to escape. She could hear them shouting and running toward her—big men dressed in white sheets with masks pulled down over their heads.

They were almost upon her. She broke out of her skis and tried to run through the snow, but it was so deep that she couldn't move. She tried to run . . . she struggled. They were gaining on her. She couldn't get away!

"Brandi? Honey, it's okay. It's just a dream. You're all right. I'm here. No one's going to hurt you."

The soft, soothing words managed to seep through her anguished mind, and Brandi opened her eyes. She'd been dreaming. The covers were wrapped around her so tightly that she couldn't move, which explained the sensation of being trapped in her dream. Tears wet her face, and she was breathing in sobbing gasps.

Greg hadn't turned on the lights, but she recognized his voice and his shadowy outline on the bed beside her.

"Greg?"

He smoothed her hair away from her forehead.

"I'm right here."

"Oh, Greg, it was so awful." Her shuddering breaths hurt her lungs.

"I know, love, I know," he murmured, gathering her into his arms and holding her close. He could feel the rapid beating of her heart against his chest. Her breathing was rapid and shallow.

Greg continued to hold her close, murmuring soothing phrases until she began to slowly relax in his arms. When he eventually loosened his hold, she stirred.

"Please don't leave me."

When Greg had heard her cry out earlier, his first thought had been to reach her side. He hadn't taken time to dress before racing up the stairs. She was still too caught up in her dream to realize that he was sitting there with very little on.

"Go to sleep, little one. Nothing's going to harm you."

"Stay with me," she whispered. "Please."

He could not resist the appeal in her voice. Knowing that he was putting a great deal of strain on his already weakened willpower, Greg mentally acknowledged this latest test of his character and crawled under the covers with her.

Brandi curled up against his chest like a kitten and sighed, arms draped around him. Despite the discomfort of having her so close and knowing he was not going to do anything about it, Greg found himself relaxing.

It felt good to hold Brandi in his arms again. He was reassured by her trust in him, even though he recognized that it might be no more than the fact that she had no one else to trust. He had learned something important that day—to take pleasure in the present moment.

He intended to do just that.

"What the hell is going on?"

Greg fought his way from a distant oblivion in order to make sense of the noise that seemed to be filling his head. He forced his eyes open and saw a dangerously irate redheaded man standing by the side of the bed. Greg's eyes drifted closed. He felt as though he'd just managed to fall asleep, and now there was someone— He shot up in the bed. "Tim! When did you get here?" He glanced around and saw that Brandi was still sound asleep, although she had been curled up by his side before he'd moved.

The full picture of what Tim must have seen when he'd come up the stairs hit Greg. If Greg had any doubts about the conclusions that Tim had drawn, he had only to look at the ominously cold stare coming from his friend's normally smiling blue eyes.

Tim Walker was a few inches short of six feet tall, but no one meeting him ever thought of him as small. His wide shoulders, muscled arms and broad chest created the image of a man you wouldn't want to tangle with. Greg glanced down at his watch. It was five o'clock in the morning, certainly not a time he'd choose for a confrontation with Tim Walker when he was upset.

Greg hastily headed downstairs to where he'd left his clothes. "I can explain—"

"You're damn right you will," Tim growled, following closely on his heels. He stood with his hands hanging loosely at his sides while Greg dressed more quickly than he had since he'd left the military.

"This isn't what it looks like."

"It's exactly what it looks like, and you know it. My God! All the years I've known you, and I had no idea you could take advantage of someone as sheltered and protected as Brandi. I could tell by her messages that she was frightened, but I knew she'd be safe up here. Hah! That's a laugh, isn't it?''

"Lower your voice, will you, before you wake her up? I haven't hurt your precious Brandi. She's fine." He strode into the kitchen and began to make coffee. "What are you doing here at this hour, anyway?"

"Oh, so it's my fault for coming early enough to catch you in bed with her, is that it? What I don't know makes everything okay, is that the way your mind works? Good God, Greg, I knew you were ruthless, I knew you could annihilate an opponent in a courtroom, but I never thought you would take advantage of a man's hospitality and seduce an innocent woman!"

"She isn't some sixteen-year-old child, for God's sake! Brandi Martin is a grown woman, Tim, a consenting adult. It is none of your damned business what we did or did not do, might or might not do, and I resent your unfounded accusations and unsubstantiated claims regarding my character!"

If Tim wanted a fight, he was going to have one, Greg decided. Some of Tim's comments had hit extremely close to the mark, echoing some of Greg's earlier thoughts, which only made him angrier. He *hadn't* taken advantage of her, even though he'd had every opportunity. He *hadn't* abused his friend's hospitality or his trust, and he was furious that he should be judged so harshly on such flimsy and circumstantial evidence.

He faced Tim, waiting for him to make the first move.

Tim leaned against the counter and stared at Greg for several tense moments without moving. Then he straightened and took a step toward him.

"Has anyone ever told you how adorable you are when you're angry?"

Greg had been ready for anything but that. He stared at his friend in astonishment. Tim was grinning. Bewildered at the sudden change in Tim's mood, Greg just stood there looking at him.

Tim began to laugh at the expression on Greg's face. "You're right, Greg. It's none of my business what you and Brandi choose to do. I guess I've looked out for her for so long that I forgot that I can't live her life for her, or make her choices for her. As you said, she's a grown woman."

Tim walked over and poured two cups of coffee, handing one to Greg. "I'm sorry for making such a fool of myself. My only excuse is that I was really worried about Brandi, which is why I drove all night to get here. When I first saw your car outside I felt nothing but relief, knowing that if you were here she was all right. To say that I was surprised at your sleeping arrangements is putting it mildly."

"You may have noticed that I was sleeping downstairs earlier."

Tim sat down at the table with a soft sigh of pleasure. "I don't mind telling you I'm tired, which partially explains why I was less than my normally observant self. Instead of my continuing to make erroneous guesses, why don't you just tell me what's going on?"

Greg sat down across from him. "Brandi's had a real scare, and I think she's still dreaming about it. I heard her last night and went upstairs to check on her. Later, after she had calmed down a little, I started to leave. She asked me to stay with her. So I did."

"And that's it?"

"That's it."

"You mean I'm not going to get to give the bride away?"

Greg studied Tim closely. "Would it bother you to see Brandi get married?"

"Not if she decided to marry you, old buddy. I couldn't be happier."

"You're really serious, aren't you?"

"Of course I'm serious. Why? Are you thinking about marrying her?"

"Don't be absurd. I just met her. Besides, I'm old enough to be her father. We're too different. We have absolutely nothing in common. And we're—"

"Whoa, wait a minute," Tim said, laughingly interrupting. "Talk about an avalanche of ridiculous reasons for not marrying someone. All you had to say was that you weren't interested in her, you know."

Greg raised his cup to his mouth without meeting his friend's inquiring gaze. He carefully sipped from the cup and meticulously replaced it in the exact spot where it had been. "I didn't say that."

"Yeah, I noticed."

They sat there for a while in silence, drinking their coffee and watching as the sky gradually lightened to a dull, threatening gray. The wind had steadily increased, its whistling moan around the corners of the house sounding like the wail of some long-lost soul.

After a while, Tim began to speak in a musing tone. "Brandi's family moved next to mine when we were kids. I think Brandi was still in diapers. I know she hadn't started school. Her father was a good provider, loved his wife and daughter. They were a very happy family. Unfortunately, her father died unexpectedly a few years later. The change in Brandi and her mother was really sad. It got to me, somehow. Up until then I'd led a rather self-centered existence, like most kids.''

Greg remained silent, so Tim continued. "I began to look in on them and offered to help with the chores. My folks took a more active interest in them and, over time, Brandi and her mother managed to pull out of the pain from their loss. By the time that happened, I'd already adopted my rather overprotective attitude toward both of them.'' He stopped and took a sip of his coffee. "I love Brandi, Greg, but I'm not *in* love with her. Not in the way you are.''

Greg met his friend's gaze without hesitation. "I don't know what you're talking about.''

"That's possible. You've never been one to stay in close touch with how you're feeling about things. I suppose your feelings for Brandi will hit you sooner or later.'' He stretched, got up and poured them some more coffee.

"I've already told you—''

"I know what you've already told me. You're too old, you have nothing in common. All of that's a bunch of hogwash, and you know it. Age doesn't mean a thing when you're both adults. Brandi is a warm, responsive person. She could teach you a lot about life if you'd allow her to get close enough. And you'd be good for her, as well. I think you have the ability to appreciate the subtleties in her character, even though you'd deny to your dying breath that you possess any sensitivities.''

Greg's emotions tumbled inside him like a roiling sea. Meeting Brandi had unleashed previously hidden portions of him, and Greg was having difficulty knowing how to deal with these new sensations.

At the moment, all he could do was play for time like the good strategist he was.

''I think you'd better hear about what Brandi accidentally stumbled into. From every indication, these people mean business. I have reason to believe that they may have traced her here. If so, they are professionals who are determined to get whoever they're after.''

Even though Tim recognized the suggested change of subject as the ploy it was, he knew that Greg was right. He needed to know what was happening.

By the time Greg had told him all that he knew, Tim's expression was as serious as Greg's. ''I had no idea this mess was so threatening. I thought that Brandi might have had prowlers at her home or something. She's pretty isolated, and I could understand if she'd gotten frightened enough to leave. But this!''

Tim got up and began to pace.

Greg glanced out the kitchen window. ''I think I'll go outside and look around before the weather gets any worse. I'll feel better, knowing that you're with Brandi. I didn't want to leave her here alone, but hesitated to suggest that she go with me. That damn red jacket of hers fairly screams for notice.''

''Good idea,'' Tim responded, watching as Greg slipped into his gray ski pants and jacket. ''I might try to get some sleep. I don't remember the last time I was horizontal.''

However, Tim's sleep was postponed by Brandi's appearance downstairs within half an hour of Greg's leaving the cabin.

''Tim! I didn't hear you come in.'' She had found him stoking the fire and launched herself into his arms almost before he had time to straighten and turn.

''Hi, Mouse!'' he replied, hugging her to him. ''How do you manage to get yourself into such crazy situations?'' he asked, shaking his head ruefully.

''So Greg told you what happened.'' She glanced around the room and over to the kitchen. ''Where is he, by the way?''

''Oh, he said something about skiing before the weather closed in any more.'' He yawned. ''I was too tired to even consider going with him.''

''I'm surprised he would have much energy after spending the night on this sofa. I tried to get him to take the bed, but he insisted on staying down here. I know he must have been uncomfortable, but I gave up arguing with him. Somehow I get the impression that few people win in an argument with that man.''

Tim watched her closely. It was obvious that she didn't remember Greg's going upstairs in response to her nightmare or her asking him to stay.

Brandi had been prone to nightmares for as long as he'd known her. One of the ways her mind dealt with them was to block them from conscious thought. No doubt she'd managed to block this most recent episode, as well.

''Have you eaten?'' she asked.

"No. And I'm starved. Would you care to take pity on me, or will I have to make my own breakfast?"

"I'll be glad to feed you if you'll explain to me why those men would be so angry that they would shoot at me?"

Tim followed her into the kitchen. "You're sure they actually were shooting?"

"Believe me, I recognized the sounds when I heard them. And I didn't imagine the truck that followed me, nor the men I saw at the sheriff's office."

"What sort of clothes were they wearing?"

"Some sort of white camouflage. They looked military, but I could be wrong."

"Are you sure you didn't wander onto one of the military installations?"

"Come on, Tim," Brandi said, busily whisking eggs together, "those bases are well marked, with high fences and posted notices."

"That's true."

"So what do you think?" she asked, setting a plateful of eggs, bacon and toast in front of him.

"Looks good."

"No! I mean about those men. What were they doing?"

"I have no idea."

"Can you find out?"

"I can try. But first I'd like to eat and maybe get a few hours of sleep, if that's not asking too much."

She grinned. "For you, my friend, I'll allow it."

"That's big of you," he mumbled through a bite of toast.

Brandi laughed. She folded her arms on the table and leaned on them, watching him for a few mo-

ments in silence. Then, in a casual tone that didn't fool
Tim in the least, she asked, "How long have you
known Greg?"

Tim smiled but didn't comment on her interest.
"We met overseas when we were in the service."

"Were you in the same unit or something?"

"No. Greg found me, badly injured, and helped me
get medical attention. I doubt that I would have made
it otherwise, but Greg gets irritated whenever I bring
up the incident, so I've learned not to refer to his sav-
ior tendencies."

"You mean it was dangerous for him to have helped
you?"

"Suicidal."

"And he did it anyway?"

"Yes."

"And he didn't even know you?"

"That's right."

"What sort of a man would do something like
that?"

"A very unusual one." Tim stared out the window.
"People are only now beginning to understand what
it was like in Southeast Asia back then. We were just
kids out of high school, raised on John Wayne war
movies, raring to go fight for our country. Only we
discovered when we got over there that it wasn't like
the movies at all." He slowly turned to look at Brandi.
"Most of us lost our youth over there. I did, and I
know Greg did."

Tim was quiet for a long moment, remembering.
Then he shook his head, and his gaze finally met hers.
"I'll never forget the first time I saw him after we got
back to the States. I'd lost track of him, and I wasn't

going to let him disappear from my life. Whether he liked to hear it or not, the fact remained that I'm alive today only because of the risks he took to save me. You can never forget something like that.''

Tim pushed his plate away. Brandi took it over to the sink and rinsed it, then poured him another cup of coffee. She didn't want to break into Tim's story. She could tell that thinking about those years caused him pain, but she felt that she needed to hear what he was going to say.

"The only address I had for him belonged to his parents in Virginia. So I went there. It was hard to believe that those two embittered people had produced the man I knew to be warm, compassionate and caring. They acted as though they barely remembered him. They didn't even know his address, just that he'd gone to Massachusetts to go to school.''

Tim shook his head. "It took me a while to locate him, and when I did I almost didn't recognize him. He looked years older. He was cold and very distant. In fact, his attitude toward me was similar to the one I'd run into with his parents. As though he couldn't imagine why I'd bothered to look him up.''

He sipped absently from the cup in front of him. "I wasn't accepting that sort of behavior from Greg. I'd gotten to know the man too well. Something was eating him alive, and I was determined to do what I could to help.''

"He'd enrolled at the Harvard law school and had a small garage apartment. I deliberately got him to drinking until he loosened up enough to tell me what had happened. It was worse than I thought.''

"What was it?" Brandi asked, watching Tim play with the handle of his cup.

"Greg explained to me that he was the youngest of three boys. He said he'd grown up knowing without understanding that he could never do anything to please his parents. He wasn't as smart as his oldest brother or as athletic as his other brother. His grades were never good enough, and neither were his achievements."

"How sad."

"The thing is, Greg never allowed their attitude toward him to stop him from trying to excel in order to win their approval."

When he didn't say anything more, Brandi finally prodded him. "So what happened?"

"Nam happened. Both his brothers were drafted, two years apart. When Greg's turn came before the draft board he was given a deferment because he was the only son left at home. When he told his parents about the deferment, his dad accused him of being a coward and hiding behind his brothers."

"Oh, no!"

"So Greg enlisted and ended up overseas."

Tim got up and poured himself another cup of coffee, but instead of returning to the table he began to pace in the small confines of the kitchen. "What he told me that night explained a lot of things to me, things about Greg that had puzzled me when I'd first gotten to know him. He'd been awarded several honors and medals for bravery, including the time he saved my life, but none of them seemed to mean anything to him. He brushed them off, and got irritated whenever anyone brought them up. It hit me that night that Greg had still been trying to prove that he wasn't a coward, which is ridiculous. Greg Duncan is one of the bravest, most courageous men I've met."

He paused in his pacing and picked up his cup.

"Surely his parents couldn't ignore all that he had done overseas," Brandi pointed out. "Didn't their attitudes toward him change at all?"

"His parents hadn't kept in touch with him while he was overseas, so Greg didn't find out until he returned home that both his brothers had been killed."

"How horrible! How awful for the whole family."

"Yes. Greg had loved both of them very much, even though, from what I could gather from his remarks about them over the months I was with him, they had been busy with their own lives while they were all growing up and showed only a casual interest in him. Losing them was devastating enough, but when his parents told him about his brothers' deaths they made it clear they resented the fact that he had survived while the two they had idolized had been killed."

"But that's really sick. How could they blame Greg for something over which he had no control?"

"Who knows, but obviously they did. By the time I managed to locate Greg he'd withdrawn behind a wall so thick I wasn't sure I'd ever get behind there and find the man I knew." He shook his head and sat down at the table once again. "But I couldn't walk away and leave him that way. He was my friend. He'd saved my life. Now it was time for me to do what I could to help him."

"So what did you do?"

Tim grinned. "Don't you remember? I ended up enrolling in school myself, moving in with him and spending hours over the following months in long philosophical discussions about the meaning of life and what we hoped to get out of it."

"It must have worked."

"Who knows? But we both got through the readjustment of returning to a country that was ashamed of what was happening in Asia and reflected those feelings onto those of us who had taken part in it."

They were both quiet for a while, thinking about the past. Finally Brandi shook her head. "It must have been terrible for someone as sensitive as Greg is to have to endure such callous treatments."

Tim glanced at her and smiled. "Does that mean you haven't been put off by his cold and aloof manner, Mouse? That you saw the man that hides behind that shield?"

"Well, just look at the situation now. He came to Colorado for a few days of peace and quiet. He obviously wanted to be alone, but instead he found me here. Greg could have been angry at my presence and irritated that I continued to stay. Every once in a while I've seen a glimpse of him that's intriguing, but he doesn't give much away about himself."

"I know."

"And yet he seems close to you."

"Because I broke through the barrier. I saw him when he had no defenses left against the world. I've watched as he rebuilt his life, set his goals and pursued them. I'm probably the closest friend he has. And yet we rarely see each other, except for an occasional visit here to ski or if I look him up in Missouri. We both keep heavy schedules, but we both know that we'd go to the wall for each other at any time."

"I know that feeling. You got me through some really rough periods in my life, Tim, and I'll never forget it. As you can see, you're the first person I turned to when I didn't know what to do."

He grinned. "I'm always glad to assist a damsel in distress, Mouse. The problem is that I'm not sure how we're going to deal with this situation. But I'll think of something."

Brandi's thoughts returned to Greg, and she wondered if he would ever allow her to get any closer to him. Their kiss of the night before continued to haunt her. She had been given a glimpse of the man hidden away from most of the world, the man she found so intriguing, the man she wanted to get to know better, to coax into sharing himself with another person—with her.

Chapter Five

Brandi and Tim heard a thump outside and looked around. Greg came in, stamping his feet to make sure he didn't bring in any snow.

Brandi felt her heart begin to race, and she forced herself to sit there quietly, watching him as he removed his outdoor clothes. The conversation she and Tim had been having seemed to ring in the room, and she was embarrassed at almost being caught discussing him, as though she had been spying.

Hearing Tim's story made her want to cry for the pain that Greg had endured with a great deal of stoicism for most of his life. He'd been trained from an early age to believe that he didn't deserve to be loved. For Brandi, the man was almost too easy to love. The feelings she was developing toward him were almost frightening in their intensity.

"Looks like you made it back none too soon," Tim observed, nodding toward the window.

For the first time, Brandi noticed the heavy flurry of snow swirling outside.

"I know," Greg said, pulling off his boots. He rubbed his hands together briskly. "I think I'm going to have a hot shower, then find something to eat."

Tim stood and followed him into the other room. "Did you see anything interesting while you were out?" He glanced over his shoulder at Brandi, then back to Greg.

Greg nodded his head. In a low voice he said, "I found where a four-wheel-drive vehicle had been parked up the road. Tracks led back this way."

"How many?"

"Two."

"I don't like the sound of that."

"Neither do I. However, I don't think we'll have any more company if this weather keeps up. As soon as it clears, I think we should get her out of here."

Brandi left the kitchen and joined them in the main room. "If you'd like, I could make you something to eat," she said, smiling at Greg.

The two men looked at each other in silence. Then Greg nodded. "That sounds great, Brandi. Thanks." Greg found some clothes in his bag and disappeared into the bathroom.

Tim began to pace. "I really should try to get back to Denver. There's no telling how long this might keep up."

Brandi looked at him as though he'd lost his mind. "But you just got here. You said yourself you needed some rest."

He ran his hand through his short, almost military-cut hair. "I know. But I'd like to get some queries started regarding the incident you witnessed."

"Maybe you could phone."

He thought about that for a moment. "Yeah, that might be the quickest way to go. Even so, I'll have to drive into town." He glanced at his watch. "That's what I'll do. I'll go into town, find a phone, then maybe get a room and wait this out. Are you going to feel comfortable staying up here with Greg until I can make it back up here?"

She smiled. Comfortable wasn't exactly the word that came to mind when she thought of Greg. "I'll feel perfectly safe, if that's what you mean," she said.

Tim studied her in silence for a few minutes. "What do you think of Greg?" he finally asked.

"I don't think I've ever met anyone quite like him, although there are times when he reminds me of you—in some ways."

Tim walked over and looked out at the falling snow. "That's not too surprising. We have several things in common."

Brandi wandered over to the fireplace and stood watching the flickering flames. "Now that you've shared with me some of his background, I can better understand why he's the way he is. I don't think he's ever learned how to play. I find myself wanting to teach him how."

Tim turned from the window. "Be careful, Mouse. I'd hate to see you hurt. Greg's had several years to erect a very sturdy wall between himself and the rest of the world."

"A couple of times I felt a deep loneliness in him that I really didn't understand at the time. I wanted to hold him close and to assure him that he wasn't alone," she said softly, not looking at Tim. "At other times, I felt that I must have imagined it. He appears so confident and self-assured."

"You're more perceptive than I gave you credit for, Mouse. Few people have seen the vulnerable side of him."

"Maybe it's because I can identify with the feeling. I consider myself strongly independent, and yet there are definitely times when I'm tired of fighting all of my own battles."

"Well, this is one time when you were right in looking for some assistance. It takes wisdom to realize that there's a certain strength in admitting when you need help. I'm glad you contacted me."

She went over and put her arms around his waist. "Me too. And I'm doubly glad you came."

Tim patted her awkwardly, then stepped back. "I'd better make tracks before it's too late to get off this mountain."

"And I want to make Greg something to eat. He must be starved." Brandi followed Tim into the kitchen area and watched as he bundled up for the weather. "Please be careful."

Tim grinned. "Always. I'll see you two as soon as I can, but I doubt that I'll brave the storm to get back up here today. Once I can get some inquiries going, I'll find a place to sleep and wait for some answers." He hugged her to him. "Take care. Tell Greg where I've gone."

Brandi waved and watched through the window as Tim carefully navigated the driveway out to the main road. The blowing snow drew a swift curtain between them and she turned away, going to the refrigerator and removing items. She'd never realized how much fun it could be to cook for someone. It was almost as though she and Greg were playing house.

Almost, but not quite, she reminded herself sternly.

A few moments later, she heard the bathroom door open and caught the scent of Greg's after-shave lotion. She would never smell that particular scent again without being reminded of him. Without turning around, she quickly filled a bowl with soup and sliced the sandwiches she'd made.

"Where's Tim?"

Brandi placed the food on the table before she looked up. Greg looked as good as she'd feared he would, the dark blue of his sweater emphasizing the blondness of his hair.

"He went to find a phone."

"In this weather?" Greg walked over to the window. "He must be crazy. He'll never make it back up here."

"I know. He said he'd find a place to stay in town and wait to get some answers to his inquiries." She didn't meet his eyes. "Sit down and eat while your soup is still hot."

When he didn't move, she glanced up at him. He looked grim.

"What's wrong?"

Greg wasn't about to tell her the truth—that he had counted on Tim's presence in the small cabin to help him get through the next couple of days without making a complete fool of himself.

"Nothing." He sat down and began to eat.

Brandi filled another bowl with soup and sat down opposite him. She noticed that he winced when he moved his right arm.

"What's wrong with your arm?"

"I don't know. I must have pulled a muscle in my shoulder or something."

"If you'd like, I could rub some cream on it after lunch."

He nodded, trying not to react to the thought of having her hands moving over his body. What the hell was wrong with him, anyway?

Brandi cleared the table and washed the dishes in record time, Greg decided later when she appeared in the living room while he tended the fire. She nodded matter-of-factly toward the rug and said, "Why don't you sit on the rug in front of the fire? You'll be warmer there without a shirt. I'll get the cream and be right back."

He heard her moving items in the bathroom medicine cabinet and almost hoped she wouldn't find anything, even though he knew that he needed some relief. The shoulder was steadily stiffening on him.

When she came back into the room, Brandi sat down on the sofa behind him and began to tug on his sweater. Reluctantly Greg helped her to remove the sweater, then his undershirt.

"My hands are probably going to feel cold to you," she said apologetically, rubbing them briskly together, then putting some cream on her palm.

Greg sat silently when she began to stroke his shoulder and down his arm. He forced himself to relax and tried to think of something else, anything but the fact that at the moment all he wanted to do was to turn and pull Brandi into his arms and kiss her senseless.

Eventually the heat from the cream began to seep into his muscles and he began to relax, luxuriating in the feel of her small hands touching him. After several moments of silence she paused and said, "How does that feel?"

"Much better," he answered gruffly, without looking at her. "Thanks." He reached for his shirt and sweater. He heard her move away from him.

"Would you like some coffee?" she asked from the kitchen area.

"Sounds good."

"The storm doesn't seem to show any signs of stopping."

He glanced out at the swirling white curtain on the other side of the glass and sighed. They were effectively marooned together, and Brandi didn't even appear to be bothered by that fact. She was treating him as though he were her brother.

He heartily wished he could share that attitude with her. Unfortunately, there was no way Greg could stir up any familial feelings toward Brandi!

When she brought the coffee in, Brandi sat down on the rug beside him. "Tell me more about what you do as a lawyer, Greg."

He accepted the cup from her and smiled briefly at the eager expression on her face. "It's rather boring, I'm afraid."

"I don't believe that. I'm sure you've had your share of interesting cases and intriguing trials."

He thought of an amusing incident that had happened a few weeks before and told her about it in precise and vivid detail, catching her off guard with his keen observational skills and his ability to capture and relate the incident with humor and compassion.

Before he fully realized what was happening, Brandi was drawing him out, asking gently probing questions about his life-style, his work and his personal life.

"You don't seem to have much time for anyone in your life with the schedule you keep, do you?" she finally asked after they had talked for several hours.

"You're right about that. Penny had a narrow escape."

"You still miss her, though, don't you?"

"I don't think so, no. I think of her occasionally, though, and wonder how my life might have changed if I had gone ahead and married."

"I think you're lonelier than you want to admit."

He shrugged. "Perhaps. I don't waste much time thinking about it."

"I'm surprised that you wanted to spend your leisure time alone. It seems to me that you would have preferred to go where there were people."

He grinned. "I'd be lying if I said I'm sorry that you've been here to share the cabin with me."

"You don't know how pleased I am to hear you say that. I've been feeling really guilty about crashing your party."

He lifted a cup. "Some party."

She smiled at him. "Well, when Tim returns I'll get out of your hair by catching a ride home with him."

"I could take you home when you're ready to go," he offered quietly.

She looked at him in surprise. "Why would you want to do that, Greg? You wouldn't get much skiing in around my place this late in the season."

"Because I want to get to know you better," he admitted, as though he were a little surprised at himself.

Brandi could feel herself growing warm. "There's really not much to know."

"Somehow I find that a little hard to believe, Brandi. For example, the field you've chosen to work in is most unusual. What made you decide to do marquetry?"

"When I was at school I became fascinated with the beautiful work done in woods during the Italian Renaissance, in the fifteenth and sixteenth centuries. At that time marquetry was regarded as a worthy art, equal to the finest paintings and sculptures of the time."

Brandi gazed into the fire as though searching for words to explain how she felt. "I was intrigued with the idea of pursuing this type of artistic expression. I wanted to see if I could help reclaim what was almost a lost art."

"I wish I could see some of your work."

She smiled. "I'll send you one of my more colorful boxes."

"That's one of the things that always puzzled me. How do you get the different colors in the wood?"

"Well, I buy wood in thin sheets. To get certain brilliant colors I dye the wood with a cloth dye by pressuring it in a pressure cooker. This causes the dye to penetrate the wood completely, which is necessary because I have to sand it."

Greg enjoyed watching the way the firelight highlighted the delicate bone structure of her face. Brandi obviously loved what she did. Her animation while describing it was proof of that.

"It must take a great deal of patience to work with the small pieces you'd need to form a picture," he commented.

"I suppose, but I really enjoy it. And there are special tools that help make it easier." Brandi smiled at him, her eyes dancing. "It probably doesn't make sense to a busy lawyer why someone would devote hours to forming in wood the variegated colors found in a flower's petal."

"On the contrary, I'm very much impressed. I noticed yesterday what a sharp eye you have for nature's beauty."

"I've always been fascinated by the shape and color of flowers...and limbs...grasses and shrubs...a bird's wing..." She paused, shaking her head. "It's not very profound, I'm afraid." Brandi was uncomfortable talking about herself, and she searched for something to say that would effectively turn the subject away from her. Without thinking about Greg's possible reaction, she said, "I'm so glad I've had this chance to meet you, Greg. Tim's right. You're a very special person."

His eyes narrowed slightly. "What sort of tales has Tim been spreading about me?"

Brandi shook her head. "Nothing that you need to feel ashamed of, I'm sure."

He frowned slightly, staring into the fire. "I should have known better than to leave him alone with you."

"He says you're a very private man."

Greg gave her comment some thought. "I suppose I am."

"And yet you've been very open with me," she pointed out.

"You have that effect on me. I don't understand it, nor can I explain it."

"I'm glad, Greg," she said softly. Leaning toward him, she kissed him softly on the cheek.

He turned and pulled her into his lap. Leaning back against the sofa, he looked down at her. "This is a dangerous situation, you know," he said slowly. "One of us needs to hang on to his sanity."

She smiled and stroked his cheek. "What a sensible idea. Should we draw straws and see who wins?"

He lowered his head slightly and touched his lips to hers. Raising his head a few inches, he asked, "And the winner hangs on to his sanity?"

She touched her lips to his for a brief instant and said, "No. The loser." Her arms circled his neck and she sighed, her mouth settling once more against his.

Brandi felt as though she had suffered through agonizing hours waiting to be kissed by Greg once again. She didn't understand the effect he had on her. She couldn't have begun to describe what was happening to her. All she knew was that she would be content to spend the rest of her life right where she was at this moment.

Greg felt as though he'd been fighting against the inexorable pull Brandi had on him ever since he'd awakened to find her presence a part of his vacation package. With her response, Brandi had inadvertently broken through all the barricades and restraints he'd placed between them.

A moan that was only barely audible registered Greg's capitulation to forces no longer in his control. The attraction he felt toward Brandi overrode every other consideration—of trust, of friendship, of the future. He knew that he would make love to her that night, regardless of what the morning would bring in the way of consequences.

Brandi sensed the change in his kiss. She felt possessed...claimed...branded—and never gave a thought to putting up a struggle. How could she, when this was what she wanted?

Greg eased her down onto the plush rug in front of the flickering flames. Pulling away slightly, he eased her sweater over her head, then removed the turtleneck shirt she wore for added warmth.

Her soft skin glowed with a rosy tint from the warmth and color of the fire. Brandi smiled, never taking her eyes off of Greg's face, not even when he unfastened her bra and carefully pulled it from her shoulders.

"I've never wanted to make love to anyone the way I want you," he whispered, planting tiny kisses at the base of her neck.

Brandi's hands came up, and she ran her fingers through the silkiness of his hair. "I know the feeling," she admitted.

"This is crazy," he muttered, unerringly finding the tip of her breast with his lips.

His hands lightly stroked across her back and down her spine, pressing her closer to him. Brandi slid her hands beneath his sweater and luxuriated in the feel of the taut muscles in his shoulders and arms.

His hand slid to the snap of her pants, and he hesitated. Raising his head, he listened for the sound he thought he had heard, a sound that did not blend with the others coming from outside.

Brandi slowly opened her eyes and gazed up at his flushed face. His profile was turned to her as he stared toward the front of the cabin. Gone was the lover. In his place was the instinctive animal, guarding its own.

"What is it?" she whispered.

"I'm not sure." He sat up.

Brandi hastily pulled her heavy sweater over her head, effectively covering her bare chest. Greg had tensed, ready to get to his feet, when Brandi heard something outside, as well. He moved swiftly into the kitchen on silent feet.

A sudden pounding started up at the door, and Brandi discovered that her heart was pounding erratically somewhere in the vicinity of her throat. Glancing around, she saw her bra and undershirt where Greg had tossed them earlier. She quickly gathered them up and stuffed them beneath the sofa cushion.

Brandi couldn't imagine who would be out on a night like this. Were they looking for her? What could she do? Where could she possibly hide? Then she re-laxed slightly. Greg was there. He wouldn't let any-one harm her. She knew that with a certainty that needed no explanations.

She stood in front of the fireplace and watched as Greg walked over to the kitchen door and opened it.

When Greg saw the two snow-covered shapes standing on the deck, he stepped back and motioned them inside. They stumbled in. Whoever they were, the storm had gotten the best of them. Their ill-advised decision to be out had almost been the death of them.

They could barely move, and Greg began to pull their overcoats and gloves off. As soon as their coats were removed, he saw an insignia on one of their shoulders. They wore uniforms.

Glancing around at Brandi, he noted that she was still hovering by the fire. This was no accident, and he knew it. Something must have been very important for these two to have braved the elements. He only had a few minutes in which to decide how best to deal with the present situation.

"Not quite the night I would have chosen for a stroll, gentlemen," he said quietly, watching as the men sank down heavily on either side of the kitchen table.

"We got lost," one of the men finally said through wheezing breaths.

"I see." Greg saw a great deal more. They wore state police uniforms. These were not military men after all. He relaxed fractionally. "How about a cup of coffee? And you might find it warmer in by the fire."

"I need to thaw out a little before I get closer to any warmth," the other man said with a grimace. "My name is Pete Phillips and my partner is Jim Stanley. We're sorry to have disturbed you, Mr.—"

"Duncan. Gregory Duncan."

"Mr. Duncan. But believe me, seeing your light probably saved our lives."

The two men began to pull off their snow boots, then briskly rubbed their hands, trying to improve their circulation.

"What brought you men up into the mountains in weather like this?" Greg asked, placing a cup in front of each one.

After taking a welcome sip of coffee, Jim replied, "We got an urgent communication from Denver to be on the lookout for a dangerous suspect."

"Oh? And you thought he might be in this area?"

"She. We were told that she'd been traced to this area, yes."

Greg glanced across the counter that divided the main room from the kitchen and saw the apprehensive look on Brandi's face.

"Who are you looking for? And what has she done?"

"Her name is Brandi Martin. She's wanted for questioning. Once apprehended, she'll be returned to Denver."

"I see." Casually leaning against the counter, Greg said, "What does she look like?"

"We don't have much to go on at the moment—a description from a driver's license. Five-one, ninety-eight pounds, blue eyes, black hair. That could describe several people," Jim muttered. He glanced into the other room and saw Brandi standing in front of the fire. He froze.

"Oh, please forgive my lack of manners," Greg said, straightening, knowing that he was taking an irrevocable step. "This is my wife, Beth. We live in Payton, Missouri. We come here to ski whenever we can find the time." Greg reached into his pocket and pulled out his wallet and handed them a card.

Pete studied it carefully. "An attorney, are you?"

"That's right." Greg smiled.

"How long have you and your wife been here?"

He glanced over at Brandi. "I'm not sure. Are you, darling? Close to a week, I'd say." He shrugged. "I lose track of time when we're out like this. The days sort of run together."

Brandi felt frozen into immobility. These men were actually out searching for her, determined to take her back with them.

Greg's glib explanation had sounded so natural. He had poured himself a cup of coffee and seemed to be interested in what they had to say, though not unduly so. His acting skills amazed her. She wasn't certain she was going to be able to handle herself as well.

"You must be hungry. How long have you been out?"

"Since noon, but we have provisions with us," Pete explained. "The thing is, we turned onto a back road and got stuck. We radioed for help and were told that the roads were closed up this way. They also said that we'd find a few homes up here that would be able to provide some shelter until morning." He shook his head. "I was beginning to wonder. We haven't seen anything."

"You were fortunate that you saw our light," Greg said quietly.

Jim nodded. "No one is worth risking our lives over."

Greg glanced out at the storm. "Well, you're safe now. We've only got the one bed, but there are extra sleeping bags, and I'm sure you'll be comfortable down here in front of the fire."

He walked into the other room and put his arm around Brandi's shoulders. "Why don't you go ahead and get ready for bed, love? I'll be up shortly, after I've made sure that Pete and Jim are made comfortable."

Brandi forced herself to smile up at him. "That's a good idea. I am rather tired."

He squeezed her shoulder reassuringly. "We'll probably find the storm over by morning and will be able to get in some more skiing."

Greg watched as Brandi disappeared into the bathroom.

"We really appreciate your hospitality, Mr. Duncan," Pete said, padding into the living room in his heavy socks.

"Call me Greg. There's no problem, officer. Glad we were able to help." He went to the closet that had been built under the stairs and pulled out two down-filled sleeping bags. "Hope these will be all right for you."

"At this point, I think I could sleep on a bed of nails," Jim admitted. "That walk really took it out of me."

By the time Brandi came out of the bathroom, the men were settled in front of the fire, chatting. She paused uncertainly. Greg glanced at her and smiled. "I'll be up in a while, darling. Good night."

"Good night," she murmured softly, then climbed the stairs.

Once again she and Greg were going to share the bed upstairs. It was beginning to be a habit. Brandi couldn't help but remember what their visitors had interrupted. She had been in a wonderfully sensuous sea of sensation. Their sudden arrival and intentions felt like a load of ice being dumped on her. She was still shaking from the transition.

She wasn't an actress. Brandi had no idea how long she could pretend that their visit was nothing out of the ordinary. One slip and all her running would have been in vain.

Brandi hated to contemplate what she would have done if Greg hadn't been there. Would she have gone with Tim? Surely he wouldn't have let her stay there alone, even though all of them had figured that she would be safe at the cabin.

What in the world had she seen that could create a statewide hunt for her? Her only hope lay in Tim's ability to get to the bottom of it as rapidly as possible.

In the meantime, the only other danger she faced was the fear that she had lost her heart to Greg Duncan. Unfortunately, Brandi recognized, it was too late to worry about that.

Brandi crawled into bed and waited for Greg to come upstairs and join her.

Chapter Six

Greg felt as though he'd become two people in the past couple of hours—one who conversed with the two police officers and another who objectively monitored the scene. He was distantly aware of the fact that his heart was racing in his chest and that his adrenaline level had risen to unbelievable heights.

While the first part of him made sure his guests were comfortable, the other swiftly and inexorably catalogued the fact that for the first time in his adult life he had willfully and most deliberately stepped outside the law. He had lied to representatives of the very justice system that he had dedicated his life to supporting.

When he'd seen the possible threat to Brandi, he hadn't hesitated to protect her, regardless of the fact that in doing so he was compromising his integrity.

Of course, the whole thing was a mistake. Whatever she had stumbled into had political overtones, of that he was certain. She was no criminal. He was counting on the fact that if anyone could quickly get to the bottom of the situation, it was Tim. Brandi only had to wait for Tim to clear up the matter.

So why had Greg lied?

The answer astounded him. While inviting his guests to make themselves comfortable and bidding them good-night, Greg came face-to-face with the realization that in the space of two short days Brandi Martin had become more important to him than his own sense of right and wrong. The strong protective feelings sweeping over him were like nothing he'd ever felt before. But he recognized the strange feelings that had overcome him, changing his life.

He loved her.

He, Gregory Duncan, who took pride in the fact that he never made a decision without carefully analyzing all his options, had allowed his feelings to sweep away all thought of the possible consequences if these men discovered that he had lied to them and was at that very moment concealing the identity of a wanted suspect.

Given the same circumstances, he would do it again without hesitation.

Was this what love was all about—doing everything in his power to protect Brandi? Feeling the need to go to her side to hold her and reassure her that he would not allow anyone or anything to harm her?

What had happened to him in these few short days that he could ignore his training, his background, his way of life, in order to make sure that Brandi was all right? What mystical powers had transformed him in such a fashion?

As Greg said good-night to his guests and started up the stairway, he humbly and silently acknowledged a power he'd never been aware of—the power of love.

The overwhelming and astonishing power of love.

Acknowledging to himself how he felt about Brandi gave Greg a sense of freedom and joy that he'd never before experienced. He felt such a wealth of emotion wash over him that he wasn't sure he could contain his reaction. Yet he knew he must.

When he reached the loft area, Greg noted that Brandi had left on the bedside lamp for him. He also noted with a grin that she was lying as far on her side of the bed as she could get without falling off, with her back turned to him.

Without saying anything, he quickly shed his clothes and crawled beneath the covers to her side. Then he reached over and turned off the light, absorbing the silent darkness while he carefully sorted through his suddenly inadequate vocabulary to find the words to tell Brandi about his recent and amazing discovery.

"Brandi?" he said softly. "Are you awake?"

A slight glow of light from downstairs enabled him to watch her as she slowly rolled over onto her back, turning her head to look at him. The faint light revealed that she had been crying, and he felt a pang in the region of his heart.

"Did you really think I could drift off to sleep without a worry?" she asked in a low voice.

"They're nice guys. You don't have to worry about them."

"I'm sure they're nice enough, to the vacationing lawyer and his wife. I have a hunch their attitudes would change if they were to learn the truth."

"They won't," he said emphatically.

She noted the grim expression around his mouth and decided that she much preferred having Greg Duncan on her side. He would make a formidable adversary. No doubt there were many attorneys in the St. Louis and Payton areas who had discovered that fact.

"Try to get some rest," he said, studying her.

She smiled. "This is becoming a habit, sharing a bed with you."

Without returning her smile, he replied, "What would you think about the idea of making it permanent?"

Her eyes widened slightly. "Making what permanent?"

"Our sleeping together."

"I'm not at all sure that I understand what—"

"I want to marry you."

His calm statement did nothing to help her comprehend what was happening between them. She knew that they had both been under considerable tension these past few days, but she could think of nothing that had happened that would cause him to suddenly make such a statement.

"Greg, you can't be serious," she said, conscious of the need to keep her voice down. The one thing neither of them wanted was to be overheard discussing marriage by the men downstairs.

"I am."

"But you can't be. You don't know me. I don't know you. A few days together isn't enough time to make a decision of that importance."

"I'm well aware of all the logical reasons, Brandi. I'm telling you how I feel. I don't want you walking out of my life. I want to marry you. I want to take you back to Payton with me. I want to know that you're safe and protected from anything life might throw your way."

Brandi could not control the trembling that overtook her at his words. The thought had never occurred to her that Greg would offer her marriage. They were both wary of getting close to anyone—of that she was certain.

As far back as Brandi could remember, she had felt that she would never marry. She wasn't sure when she had first made up her mind about that. Perhaps when her father had died and she'd seen the devastation his loss had caused to her mother and, to a lesser degree, herself.

She felt as though she had learned a valuable lesson at a very young age—it was not healthy to be dependent on another person. Brandi had accepted that belief and learned to live with it, and that had helped her later to survive the loss of her mother.

She had learned to live alone, to take care of herself—most of the time, at least. Recent events had certainly caused her to question her ability to take care of herself.

For some reason she had thought that Greg understood and even agreed with her philosophy of life. He had seemed to be content with his solitary existence.

WOW!

THE MOST GENEROUS
FREE OFFER EVER!
From Silhouette® Books

GET 4 FREE BOOKS WORTH $7.80

Affix peel-off stickers to reply card

NO COST! NO OBLIGATION!
NO PURCHASE NECESSARY!

Because you're a reader of Silhouette romances, the publishers would like you to accept four brand-new Silhouette Romance™ novels, with their compliments. Accepting this offer places you under no obligation to purchase any books, ever!

ACCEPT FOUR BRAND NEW
YOURS

We'd like to send you four free Silhouette® novels, worth $7.80 retail, to introduce you to the benefits of subscribing to Silhouette Books. We hope your free books will convince you to subscribe, but that's up to you. Accepting them places you under no obligation to buy anything, but we hope you'll want to continue!

So unless we hear from you, once a month we'll send you six additional Silhouette Romance™ novels on free home approval. If you choose to keep them, you'll pay just $1.95 per volume. And there is no charge for shipping and handling! There are *no* hidden extras! And you may cancel at any time, for any reason, and still keep your free books and gifts, just by dropping us a line!

ALSO FREE!
ACRYLIC DIGITAL CLOCK/CALENDAR

As a free gift simply to thank you for accepting four free books we'll send you this stylish digital quartz clock — a handsome addition to any decor!

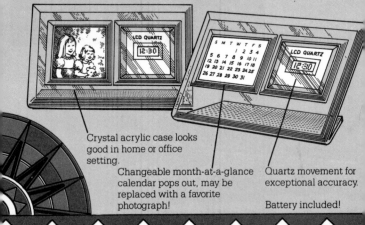

Crystal acrylic case looks good in home or office setting.

Changeable month-at-a-glance calendar pops out, may be replaced with a favorite photograph!

Quartz movement for exceptional accuracy.

Battery included!

WE EVEN PROVIDE FREE POSTAGE!

It costs you *nothing* to send for your free books — we've paid the postage on the attached reply card. And we'll pick up the postage on your shipment of free books and gifts, and also on any subsequent shipments of books, should you choose to become a subscriber. Unlike many book clubs, we charge *nothing* for postage and handling!

She placed her hand on his cheek and stroked it softly, enjoying the feel of his slightly rough skin. "That's very kind of you," she said quietly. "But it isn't necessary. And it certainly isn't wise."

Her loving touch and soft tones were in contradiction to her words, and Greg stared at her in bewilderment.

"I didn't propose because I was being kind, Brandi," he pointed out dryly. "I proposed because I love you and want to marry you."

"Not really," she contradicted in a reasonable tone of voice. "You're feeling this way because we've been alone together here. Once you return home you'll wonder what you ever saw in me."

Greg could feel his irritation at her matter-of-fact explanation of his feelings. "Brandi, I'm old enough to know myself, what I want, and how I feel. I love you. I want to marry you." As if to prove a point, he pulled her into his arms and kissed her.

His kiss was filled with a possessive fervor, as though he were determined to prove to her that his feelings were authentic.

Brandi discovered that no matter how logically she viewed their situation, as soon as Gregory began to kiss her, all thoughts flew out the window. The only thing she was aware of was how he made her feel.

Greg knew by her response to him that she was far from indifferent to him. Why didn't she know that? How could she possibly ignore what they experienced together? Every time he touched her, spontaneous combustion occurred.

Didn't that count for something?

He pulled away slightly and gazed down at her. "I want you to marry me," he said fiercely in a low voice.

"No."

"You can't mean that."

"Take my word for it. I mean it."

"Do you realize that if I wanted to I could make love to you right this minute?"

"Isn't that what you've been doing?"

"Honey, I haven't begun to show you what I intend to do when we make love."

"Just for the record, counselor, I'd like to point out that the evidence shows I am putting up absolutely no struggle. There's been no force used in this seduction."

He jerked away from her and sat up in bed, running his hand through his hair. "Damn it, Brandi. You're making fun of me. And I've never been more serious in my life."

She obligingly sat up beside him and said, "I believe that's one of the problems here. You take everything seriously, Greg. Where's your sense of humor?"

"What are you talking about?"

"Well, here we are having a debate—whispering, of course, so those two downstairs won't discover that I'm the woman they're searching for—on the possible merits of a marriage that you've already told them took place."

"You find that humorous?"

"I'd rather laugh about it than cry."

Greg realized that Brandi was unaware that he'd seen her slightly swollen eyes and tearstained cheeks when he'd first come to bed. Obviously she wasn't going to admit to giving in to tears. She wasn't even going to admit that she needed him—or anybody else, with the exception of Tim.

He should feel ashamed of himself for taking advantage of the situation. He should; but he didn't.

"Brandi, we both know that eventually we'll get to the bottom of whatever's going on in the hills near your home. As soon as Tim comes back he'll know what actions will be the most sensible for you to take. I'm not trying to rescue you, for God's sake. I want to marry you."

She was quiet for several minutes. "I really believe that you believe that statement."

"Damn it!" He paused, then consciously lowered his voice. "You can be very irritating. Has anyone ever pointed that out to you before?"

She smiled. "Oh, yes."

"Good. Then it probably doesn't come as a complete shock to you that I've mentioned it."

"No. That's just one of the reasons I'd never consider getting married. You see," she explained in a confidential tone, "I don't want to ever have to worry that my being irritating is going to create a problem in someone's life. Now they can get away from me until they get over it."

"This may come as a real blow to your theory, my love, but finding you irritating does not make me want to marry you any less."

"It doesn't?"

"No."

"Oh."

"You see, you have all sorts of personality quirks that I find endearing—lovable, actually. Irritating I can live with."

"You just don't understand, Greg. It isn't as though I don't like you. I do. Very much. And I'm very attracted to you."

"Well, thank God for small blessings."

"But that isn't enough on which to base a good marriage."

"It's a damn good start."

"What I mean is, I'm not marriageable material."

"What's that supposed to mean?"

"Some women grow up knowing that they will eventually become wives. I've always known I wouldn't. Therefore, I've never made any effort to find out what it would take to be a good wife. Take my word for it, Greg. You're going to look back on this night as one of the narrowest escapes you ever had." She stretched out on the bed once more and sighed. "I hadn't realized how tense I was. Thanks for talking to me. It's really helped me to relax." She plumped her pillow and turned over. "Good night, Greg."

He stared at her, dumbfounded. She was through talking. She had found their discussion relaxing, for God's sake. She had turned down his proposal of marriage as though he'd offered a second helping of dessert, and she'd refused in the same manner as she would have dessert, explaining it wasn't good for her.

What kind of woman was she, anyway?

Greg lowered himself to the bed and stared at her back. Was she right? Had he just had a narrow escape? After all, what sort of life would he have with a woman like that? Didn't she understand what he was offering her—a stable home life, a devoted husband, a *wealthy*, devoted husband...a boring, workaholic husband?

She knew. A couple of days in his company had shown her what a narrow existence he led. He didn't really blame her. He'd made no effort these past few years to do more than work.

Greg lay there for hours and faced the kind of person he had become. He didn't like what he saw. He didn't like it at all.

When had he become so set in his ways? So inflexible? So pompous? Why had he thought that a proposal of marriage from him would be immediately and gratefully accepted? He didn't have the foggiest idea how to be a part of a relationship. Perhaps that was why he spent so much of his time working. He was comfortable practicing law. He knew what to do and he was good at what he did. There was a sense of accomplishment and purpose, tangible evidence that he was a success at something.

He didn't know how to relate to another person.

When he'd met Penny he'd been drawn to her warmth and her even disposition. He had visualized them establishing a companionable marriage—with no unexpected scenes or surprises. When her childhood sweetheart had turned up just before their wedding, Greg had been given the opportunity to see a whole new side of Penny, one that he hadn't known existed. Rather than deal with his discovery, he had walked away from the situation.

Walking away from emotional situations had always been his way of handling them. Now he didn't want to walk away. He wanted to explore these new emotions, to come to terms with them, to incorporate them into his world.

Greg felt as though his life had gone from black-and-white photography to living color. The color was dazzling, almost blinding in its intensity. He needed help in coming to terms with the full spectrum before him.

He felt as though meeting Brandi had snapped him out of that colorless, emotionless world. Even his irritation had been surprising. As a rule, he was adept at not letting his feelings surface. He'd always had the ability to present his case effectively.

Now he'd tried to win the most important victory of his life, and he'd blown it completely.

He forced himself to relax, closing his eyes. All right, so he'd blown it. He'd asked and she'd turned him down. She hadn't really believed he was serious—and if he was, she wasn't interested.

He couldn't blame her. He didn't have much to offer in the way of companionship...love...excitement. But he intended to learn as quickly as possible. He certainly wasn't going to give up. Now that his goal was within sight, Greg knew that he was going to do whatever it took to win Brandi Martin.

As he was dozing off to sleep he felt her curl up to the warmth of his back, her arm curving around his waist. He smiled to himself. Awake, Brandi might not think they had a future together, but asleep she was already making it clear that she was comfortable having him nearby.

When Brandi opened her eyes the next morning she was dazzled by the brilliant light coming from outside. She raised up on her elbow and gazed out the bedroom window. New snow lay everywhere in drifts, the sunlight catching glints of sparkle in the pristine white mounds.

The storm was over.

She could see small animal tracks crisscrossing the hillside, and she smiled. It would be a perfect day to go out and explore.

Then she remembered.

The two police officers had spent the night. Greg had once again shared her bed. He had proposed to her. She sank back under the covers and pulled them up to her ears. Perhaps she wasn't as ready to face the new day as she'd first thought.

Brandi listened for voices from downstairs, but she could hear nothing. She could only smell the tantalizing aroma of fresh coffee, which was enough to give her courage to crawl out of bed.

She felt rested, which surprised her. For some reason she seemed to sleep better when Greg was there in bed with her than when she slept alone. She couldn't understand it. She certainly wasn't used to sleeping with anyone else. How was it possible that she could sleep so deeply, without dreaming, and not be disturbed by his presence?

Brandi shrugged and crawled out of bed. She found the heavy velour robe she'd purchased during their last trip to town, slid her bare feet into her warm fleece-lined house slippers and made her way downstairs.

She paused at the bottom of the stairs. There was no sign of their previous night's guests. The room looked neat and clean, and there was a fire dancing merrily in the fireplace. The coffee was warming in an empty kitchen. She poured herself a cup and sat down at the table.

Glancing out the window, she could see that Greg had been busy since he'd gotten up. The porch and stairs had been shoveled clean and a path had been dug to the car. Squinting slightly against the glare, Brandi spotted Greg clearing the drive to the cabin.

On sudden impulse, she decided to join him. She finished her coffee quickly, then, after dressing into her ski clothes, let herself outside.

What a glorious day. It was crisp and clear, with no sign of wind. She didn't feel the cold through her warm clothing. Brandi wanted to laugh out loud with the sheer joy of being alive and able to experience this latest miracle of nature.

Greg glanced up, and she waved. He waved back and began to walk toward her. His proposal from the night before popped into her head, and all at once she wondered how she was supposed to treat him now. She'd never had anyone propose to her before, and she wasn't certain of the proper etiquette in such a situation.

She hadn't wanted to hurt him. In some unconscious way she knew that she was actually protecting herself by refusing to even consider the idea. What she had said the night before was true. She'd never considered the possibility that someday she might meet someone who would change her mind about marriage.

It wasn't the institution of marriage she was avoiding as much as it was the long-term intimacy that marriage suggested. Greg had implied that she had been willing to make love to him, and he'd been correct, even though she still couldn't explain her reaction to him.

Brandi had never been tempted to make love with anyone before. She'd never allowed anyone the opportunity to get through her defenses. Somehow Greg had. No doubt the frightening situation she'd run from had already shaken her so that she hadn't been able to rebuild her defenses by the time she'd awakened and discovered him in bed with her.

Whatever the cause, she had allowed Greg more liberties than she'd ever allowed another man—and she'd thoroughly enjoyed every minute of it.

But that didn't mean that she could be a wife to him, or that she had the foggiest understanding of what he might expect from her as a wife.

"Good morning."

Brandi realized that the man had an unfair advantage. The combination of his flashing smile, dancing eyes and seductively low voice played havoc with all her good intentions to spare him a future with her.

"Hi."

Brandi couldn't think of anything else to say. She just stood there and looked up at him, enjoying the sight of him along with the rest of nature's miracles.

"Did you sleep well?"

She nodded. "What happened to the police officers?"

He glanced back to the road, which curved out of sight around the hillside. "They heard the snowplow out early this morning and went to catch up with it. They've had time to get their car unstuck and back to town by now." He dropped his arm companionably around her shoulders, the snow shovel in his other hand, and started walking back up to the cabin. "I don't know about you, but I'm starving."

Greg didn't want to tell her that when he'd awakened that morning, just past dawn, he'd had the worst struggle of his life not to make love to her. She had felt so natural there in his arms, and he'd wanted her so badly that he still ached with it. But making love wasn't going to settle the questions between them.

He'd gotten up and made coffee for himself and Pete and Jim, seen them off and decided to start clearing the driveway. Greg could only hope Tim would make it back that day. His sense of honor and his willpower had never before been so tested.

Greg had spent the intervening hours looking at himself, his life and his goals. He had realized that if he didn't like what he saw, he could change it. He was in control of his life. He accepted full responsibility for the restricted, shallow existence he'd chosen up until the time he had met Brandi.

With firm resolve, he was determined to change . . . not because of her but because of what he wanted out of life. He wanted a full, substantial, loving relationship. He wanted a family. He wanted sons and daughters with curly black hair and big blue eyes in elfin faces. He wanted to be there for them, to watch them grow, to listen to their stories, to share in their triumphs and their disappointments.

No longer was he willing to settle for the tepid companionship that he had thought he wanted with Penny. With Brandi he knew that he could have a Technicolor spectacular of a marriage—filled with fireworks, crashing cymbals and rooms filled with love and laughter.

All he had to do was to convince her of that.

A piece of cake.

Chapter Seven

Breakfast became a hilarious affair. Brandi wasn't sure what had caused the difference, but Greg seemed to be lighthearted, teasing her unmercifully with outrageous suggestions for breakfast.

She ended up preparing *huevos rancheros*, a Mexican dish of scrambled eggs and chopped beef wrapped in a flour tortilla and covered with a hot sauce. Brandi was determined to show him that despite his ridiculous suggestions she could turn out a breakfast that was neither dull nor boring.

"My God, my tongue is on fire," he said after a few bites. He grabbed his glass of orange juice.

"I told you not to be so liberal with the hot sauce," she pointed out calmly, continuing to eat.

"You also said it wasn't all that hot."

"I told you the bottle was labeled Medium Spicy. But if you aren't used to it, the sauce can seem rather hot."

"You can say that again." He tentatively took another bite. "Great flavor, though."

"But not what you'd expect a lawyer to have for breakfast on a daily basis."

He grinned, wiping his mouth with a napkin. "Oh, I don't know. I have a hunch it might give me an unusual amount of energy to meet the demands of a busy schedule."

Brandi unobtrusively tried to study him at odd moments, wondering why he seemed so different today. He was dressed in a heavy sweater and winter pants, his usual attire since she'd known him. The morning exercise had given him a ruddy color that was in attractive contrast to his light hair.

The change seemed to be from within. It was as though he glowed with an inner light. He seemed more relaxed, somehow. There were no distractions today. He was totally and completely focused on her. She found the attention a little unnerving. It was almost as though he were a missile locked in on a target. Brandi had an uneasy suspicion that she was the target.

She hadn't brought up his proposal of the night before. Neither had he. Brandi supposed she was relieved that he wasn't going to try to debate the issue with her. She reminded herself once again that he would be a formidable foe. She had no desire to cross swords with him.

If you lost this battle, you'd probably find yourself married to him, she reminded herself. A shiver ran down her backbone at the thought.

"Are you cold?" he asked, getting up and pouring them some more coffee.

"No."

"Good. I was hoping I could talk you into going skiing after we give our breakfast a chance to settle."

She grinned. "I'd love it. I just wish I'd brought my camera. Today looks like a winter wonderland."

Greg sat down across from her again and picked up his cup. "I can't help wondering if we'll hear from Tim today."

"He said he'd get back to us as soon as he learned anything."

"I know you'll be glad to have this nightmare behind you."

She nodded.

"I've been thinking. Why don't you come back to Payton with me? No one would question your presence there. You'd be safe while you wait until this mess is resolved."

She was quiet for a few minutes, thinking over his suggestion. He'd been casual enough in his offer, in much the same way she imagined he'd have made such an offer to Tim.

Now that she knew she had been traced to this area, Brandi knew she couldn't stay there.

But would she feel any safer with Greg at his home? He had an unusual effect on her. All her lifelong convictions seemed to waver and wilt whenever he was around.

"I might consider it, on one condition," she finally said.

"Name it."

"There will be no discussion of marriage between us."

"Whatever you say," he replied immediately.

"Because you know how I feel about the idea."

"Not really. All I know is that you don't consider me ideal marriage material."

"I never said that!"

"That's the impression I got."

"Well, I never even implied that. I'm sure you'll make someone a fine husband, if that's what you really want. I'm just saying that you don't know me well enough to want to marry me."

His grin widened. "Then I find it very accommodating of you, Ms. Martin, to allow me the opportunity to get to know you better."

"Wait a minute. That's not what I meant." Why was she having so much trouble explaining something so simple? "I don't mind getting better acquainted with you. I would like to be your friend, Greg. I just don't want more than that."

"I see."

"Somehow I doubt it."

"What you're saying is that you will come and stay with me for a few days until Tim lets us know you can go home safely only if I treat you as a friend and not as a potential mate."

"That's it. You've got it."

"I can live with that."

"Good."

"Can you?"

"What do you mean by that?"

"I suppose that only time will tell. Why don't we get some skiing in while we're waiting to hear from Tim?

Who knows? He may be able to get to the bottom of it immediately and we can go our separate ways, content to mail Christmas cards to each other annually.''

She looked at him through narrowed eyes. "Are you making fun of me?"

"Of course not! Why do you ask?"

"Because you're smiling."

He immediately stopped smiling. Looking at her sternly, he asked, "Is that better?"

"Your eyes are smiling."

He grinned. "You're adorable. Has anyone ever told you that?"

She shook her head. "Mostly I'm told that I'm irritating, stubborn, opinionated, too independent and a pain in the posterior."

He stood and pulled her up with him. "Then I've got a great deal to look forward to, haven't I? Just think, by the time I see all those sides of your personality I'll be eternally grateful that you refused to marry me."

As she pulled on her outdoor clothes once again, Brandi couldn't help but realize that she rather resented his cheerful assessment of their present relationship.

Hours later they returned to the cabin, happily exhausted, and saw Tim's car. Brandi breathlessly shed her skis and stumbled up the stairs and across the deck to the door.

"Tim?" she called, throwing open the door. "What did you find out?" She bent over and started unlacing her boots.

She heard a noise from the couch, and Tim's frowning face appeared over the back of it. "I found out that I might as well forget about catching up on my sleep if you're anywhere in the vicinity," he grumbled, running his hand through his hair.

Brandi stepped out of her boots and padded over to where he sat stretching.

"Well? What did you find out?" she demanded.

Tim glanced around. "Where's Greg?"

"Oh, he's coming. We were out skiing. Isn't it a gorgeous day?"

He narrowed his eyes when he looked toward the bright expanse of snow and sky. "Yeah. Gorgeous."

"C'mon, Tim. Tell me."

"I only want to explain once, and I need Greg's opinion on a couple of things." He stood and dropped his arm around her shoulder. "So, Mouse, have you been behaving yourself while I've been gone?" He began to walk toward the kitchen.

"Of course."

"And Greg has been the perfect gentleman, has he, chivalrously giving up the bed to you?"

"Well, not exactly. You see, we had some unexpected company last night."

Tim stopped in the kitchen and looked down at her. "Last night? In that storm? Who in the hell was out in that?"

"Two state police officers, looking for a dangerous suspect for questioning—Brandi Martin."

Tim sat down rather abruptly at the table and muttered several unprintable phrases just as Greg walked through the door.

"I resent that last remark. I know for a fact that my parents were married for several years before I was born," he said calmly, unzipping his jacket.

"I wasn't talking about you, counselor."

"Well, that certainly relieves my mind, let me tell you. Whose ancestry are you discussing?"

"I want to hear about your visitors last night."

"Oh, them," Greg said nonchalantly, pulling off his boots and walking over to the counter, where he poured himself a cup of coffee. "I don't know about you guys, but I could use something to eat. How does soup and sandwiches sound?"

"Greg, I'm serious," Tim said in an irritated tone.

"So am I. I really burn up energy when I'm skiing. Anyone else hungry?"

Brandi tried to hide her smile as she got up and began to help Greg with the meal. She'd never known anyone to give Tim Walker a hard time before—besides herself, of course. She was enjoying it immensely.

Greg glanced over his shoulder. "We could make a deal, Walker. Fill us in on any information you picked up and I'll do the same."

"Damn. I forgot about you and your negotiating skills, Duncan," Tim said with a grin. They looked at each other and burst out laughing.

Brandi felt left out of the male camaraderie for the moment and yet felt a warmth pervade her at the obvious closeness of the two men. She had a tremendous respect for Tim Walker and his judgment. There was no denying the close bond between these two men.

Within minutes they were seated and in front of them were steaming bowls of soup and a platter piled high with sandwiches. Without thinking about it, Brandi had sat next to Greg, across from Tim.

Greg nodded toward Tim. "Any information?"

"Some, but nothing conclusive. Whatever is going on up there is either supersecret or without sanction by the government. My guess is that it's both. I had to put my reputation on the line to convince some high-ranking people that what I described had actually happened."

"So what's next?" Greg asked.

Tim paused long enough to take a couple of bites of his sandwich. "Well, that's what I was going to discuss with you before I heard about your visitors," he said to Greg. "I don't want to take Brandi back to Denver with me. I thought she'd be safer staying here with you, if you would be willing to spend some extra time. Now I'm not too sure about that idea, either."

Greg smiled at Brandi. "We've been discussing that this morning. The two men who were here last night had not seen a picture of Brandi, so I introduced her as my wife, Beth."

Tim raised one brow slightly. "Your wife, Duncan? Couldn't you have been more original than that? What about your daughter?"

"Very funny." He glanced around at Brandi, who was studiously eating her soup without looking up. "Although you're probably right, I could pass as her father just as well."

Brandi choked and looked up at the two men.

"I asked her to marry me last night, but she was too polite to point out the difference in our ages."

Tim stared at his friend in disbelief. Brandi wished she could hide under the table. She couldn't remember ever having been so embarrassed. How dare he bring up his proposal so casually, and in front of Tim?

"You want to marry Brandi?" Tim said in a surprised voice.

"Well, I thought I did, but after she carefully enumerated all of her many faults, she's almost convinced me that I had a rather lucky escape." He winked at Tim.

Tim's gaze fell on Brandi's crimson face. "You turned him down?"

"He was just being polite," she managed to get out.

"That's funny, I've never thought of Gregory Duncan as particularly polite before. Must be a side of him I've never seen."

"Well, it was the third night I was going to be sleeping with her, so I thought I should at least offer—"

"Third night!" Brandi interrupted indignantly. "It was only the second night. You slept downstairs—"

"'Fraid not, Mouse," Tim interjected. "The morning I got here I found the two of you all snuggled up together."

Brandi stared at each man with dismay.

"Don't you remember the nightmare you had?" Greg asked in a low voice.

Brandi paused, thinking back. "Vaguely. I've been dreaming a lot lately."

"I heard you cry out and went upstairs to check on you. You asked me to stay."

"And I demanded that he do the proper thing and make you an honest woman. Obviously he took my advice."

Brandi threw her napkin down. "This is the most ridiculous conversation I've ever been involved in."

She glared at Tim. "It's none of your business who I sleep with!"

Tim smiled and took a sip of his coffee. Over the rim of the cup he eyed her and said, "So Greg reminded me."

"Good." She turned to Greg. "And as for you, it would have served you right if I'd said yes! Then where would you be?"

Greg's mouth twitched slightly, but he said in a solemn tone, "The possible consequences of my reckless behavior bring horror to my innermost being, Brandi. All I can say is I had the narrowest escape of my life. Thank you for your mercy." He picked up his sandwich and took a bite.

Brandi jumped up from the bench. "I hope both of you are having a marvelous time at my expense," she said in an injured tone.

Two pairs of innocent eyes turned and stared at her in puzzlement. "What did we do?" they said in unison, for all the world as though they'd practiced for hours to perfect their response.

"I'm going upstairs to take a nap," she announced, walking away.

"Try not to have any nightmares," Tim called out with a grin. "Otherwise, Greg will be upstairs forcing another proposal on you." Greg bit his lower lip to keep from laughing.

The two men were silent for a few moments after she left. Finally Greg said in an entirely different tone from the one he'd been using to tease Brandi, "What's the word?"

"I don't like it. Not at all. I was able to get in touch with the people who should know if something of that nature was going on. They were totally unaware."

"Do you believe them?"

"In this case, yes. They're men I've worked with before. They wouldn't lie to me."

"So where does all of this leave Brandi?"

"In a very vulnerable position at the moment. I was told to bring her in—for questioning."

"What?"

"Yeah. They believe *me*, all right, but they're hoping that maybe she only imagined part of what she saw."

"And I suppose she imagined the men chasing her, even to having an all points bulletin out for her arrest?"

"Calm down. I'm not turning her over to them." He studied the man across the table from him. "Care to explain what's going on with you and Brandi?"

"Obviously nothing, as far as she's concerned. But I'm not ready to give up."

"You mean you sincerely want to marry her?"

"Come on, Walker. You've known me a long time. I don't go around proposing to women out of motives of chivalry. I fully intend to marry her. But it may take a little time."

"It will take more than a little, let me warn you. Brandi's petrified of commitment. The only reason she's allowed me in her life is because she feels safe with me. I give her plenty of space, don't try to become a part of her daily existence."

"I love her, Tim."

Tim grinned. "I had a hunch that might be the case, particularly after I walked in on you the other morning."

"My overreaction was strictly due to a guilty conscience, believe me."

"Well, it sounds to me as though marriage might be the safest thing if you're going to continue sleeping with her every night."

"I haven't made love to her, Tim."

Tim leaned back and studied his friend in silence. "Why not?"

"For several reasons. One of the biggest is the fact that I didn't come prepared for such an eventuality and I have a hunch she isn't protected. I don't want to take a chance at this stage in our relationship that Brandi would feel forced into marriage with me due to an unplanned pregnancy."

"Good point."

"Well, I just wanted you to know I'm not totally without principles, old man."

"To be honest, I'd breathe a lot easier at night if I knew she was with you. I'm not sure what to do now. As soon as I get to Denver, they're going to be watching me, hoping I'll lead them to her."

"What about now? Do they know she's here?"

"No. That's why I was so surprised to hear the police had been here."

Greg threw up his hands. "Great. So now not only do we have to keep her hidden from the characters who've been chasing after her, but also from our own government officials."

"That's about the size of it."

"She's agreed to go back to Payton with me."

Tim leaned back. "That's a thought. Nobody would connect her with you."

"I don't care if they do. I still intend to marry her."

"Even after the list she gave you of all her undesirable traits?"

"Well, I'm not going to give her a list of mine, that's for sure. She can find them out on her own."

Tim grinned. "Oh, I don't know. You're not so bad. It's a shame you're not my type—I'd marry you myself."

"Has anyone ever told you what a rotten sense of humor you have, Tim?"

"It may have been mentioned once or twice. Why?"

"Never mind."

"When are you planning to leave?"

"I'd like to get on the road as soon as possible. We were waiting to hear from you before taking off." Greg glanced at his watch. "We wouldn't get too far before dark. Maybe we should wait until morning."

Tim stood. "That's up to you, but personally I feel that the sooner we get Brandi away from here, the better off she's going to be. Not too many people know about this place, but if someone was determined to find me, they could. I'd sleep better knowing she wasn't anywhere around me."

Greg stood, too. "Good point." He walked into the main room, and Tim followed. "I think I'll load up the car so Brandi can rest as long as possible."

"Has she already agreed to go with you?"

"Yes, if I don't discuss marriage with her."

Tim looked startled for a moment, then burst out laughing. "My only regret," he said when he paused for breath, "is that I won't be able to witness your courtship. Maybe you could videotape it for me."

Greg grinned. "Go to hell."

In a more sober tone, Tim replied, "No, thanks. I've already been there...and so have you." The two men looked wordlessly at each other, nodded and turned away.

When Greg went upstairs to awaken Brandi, he found her contentedly curled up under one of the heavy quilts.

"Brandi?" he said softly, sitting down beside her. She looked so peaceful, so innocent of the many undercurrents that were swirling around her. "Honey, I hate to wake you..." His voice trailed off. Leaning over, he braced his arms on either side of her and kissed her softly on the lips. Without opening her eyes, Brandi raised her arms and curled them around his neck, holding him close.

Once again, she'd been dreaming. This time, however, her dreams were far from nightmarish. She was with Greg. She knew she was safe...knew that she would always be safe...because of Greg. His kiss seemed so natural, and she pulled him closer to her, loving the feel of his body against hers.

Why had she fought her feelings for him? She loved him. She never wanted to lose him from her life. She couldn't lose him, not now. She needed him so much. She needed—

Her eyes flew open, and she realized that Greg was actually kissing her and that she was encouraging him. She stiffened, pulling away and staring up at him in alarm. What had she been thinking of? Of course she didn't need him. She didn't need anyone.

"I'm sorry to wake you," he said, "but Tim and I both feel we need to get you out of here. Are you still willing to go with me to Payton?"

She glanced toward the window. "Now?"

He nodded. "The sooner the better."

"Why?" She struggled to sit up, and he moved away from her. "What's happened?"

"Nothing new. This is just a preventive measure. There's no reason to take any chances when we don't have to."

Brandi threw back the covers and stood, then swayed, almost losing her balance. Greg reached out and braced her shoulder with his hand. "You okay?"

"I got up too quick, that's all." She started downstairs. "Is Tim still here?"

"Yes. We've been loading the car."

Brandi found that everything she'd managed to accumulate in the few days she'd been at the cabin was now packed in the car.

Tim grabbed her and held her close to him. "Take care of yourself, Mouse. I'll be in touch."

She hugged him back. "Then you think this is the best thing to do?"

"Yes." He leaned down and whispered, "I also think you should consider making an honest man out of this fellow. You've already ruined his reputation, staying with him like this. What are all of his neighbors going to think when he shows up in Payton with you as a houseguest?"

Brandi pulled away. "My God! I hadn't thought of that."

"I was only kidding."

"Maybe so, but you're right. I can't go over there and stay with Greg. Payton's a small town. What are the townspeople going to think?"

Tim grinned. "You know very well what they'll think, Mouse."

"I can't go."

"Yes, you can. But you might want to seriously consider his proposal."

"Don't be silly. He wasn't serious." She glanced around to make sure that Greg hadn't heard her. He was in the kitchen pulling out cans of drink and putting them into a Styrofoam carrying case.

"You think not? Greg doesn't joke around about things like that."

"But I can't marry him! I don't intend to marry anyone. You know that!"

"I know that has been your opinion of things for several years now, Mouse. I'd like to leave you with a thought—if you haven't changed your opinions in the past ten years, you might want to check your pulse. You may be dead."

"But, Tim, I'd make a lousy wife. I don't know the first thing about it."

"Funny you should say that. Greg feels his qualifications as a husband are equally nil. Personally, I think that's a great foundation. You don't have any preconceived notions to unlearn."

He gave her a brief hug and a kiss on the cheek. "Think about it, Mouse. Don't let your fear of the unknown stop you from fully enjoying all that life has to offer. Life is too short to deny yourself."

"Brandi, are you ready?" Greg called from the kitchen.

She looked up at Tim. "No," she whispered for his ears only. "I'm not. But I'm going anyway."

Tim grinned. "That's my girl. You can do it."

Brandi joined Greg in the kitchen. While she was pulling on her coat, the two men discussed the weather conditions and driving time, and Greg told Tim the approximate time he hoped to arrive home.

"Don't call me," Tim cautioned. "I'll call you when I have any news."

Greg nodded, understanding what Tim didn't want to put into words in front of Brandi—that his own employers would be monitoring his calls and looking for answers.

The car was running and warm inside when Brandi and Greg got in. Brandi glanced back at Tim, who stood on the deck and waved as they drove away. She didn't know what she would have done without Tim in her life. His support and encouragement carried a great deal of weight with her.

But could she take his advice? Glancing out of the corner of her eyes, Brandi took in the competent picture that Greg made driving down the narrow, winding road to the main highway.

She trusted this man with her life. Could she possibly learn to trust him with her heart?

Chapter Eight

I think I'm going to stop at the next town, Brandi," Greg said several hours later.

Brandi glanced at her watch, surprised to see how long they had been on the road.

"I'm sorry. I should have offered to drive. I was so involved in our discussion I didn't realize the time."

During the hours on the road they had covered a multitude of subjects and had discovered how many times their views coincided. Greg had been greatly encouraged to find how similar their perspectives and values were, although he doubted that Brandi had given much thought to what was happening between them.

She had debated several times with considerable spirit while Greg had played devil's advocate. He'd enjoyed her keen insight and incisive mind as she'd made her points. Whether or not she realized it,

Brandi could have put her logic and eloquence to good use in a courtroom.

"If we stop now we should get into Payton tomorrow afternoon, which will give you an opportunity to see it during the daylight."

Brandi suddenly remembered what they were doing. Greg was taking her to his home in a small town.

"How are you going to explain my presence in your home?" Brandi asked after a few moments of silence.

"I didn't intend to make explanations to anyone. Why do you ask?"

"Surely your reputation is important to you."

He grinned. "My reputation can only be enhanced by showing up with an attractive woman."

"You know what I mean. Perhaps I should stay in a motel or something."

"Nothing doing. You're going to stay with me, including tonight. I intend to register as Mr. and Mrs. Duncan. I don't want to take any chances with you."

"Surely that's not necessary."

"Tim and I feel it is. Since you've allowed us to help you, I think you should follow our advice."

He pulled into a driveway near the famous logo of a national motel chain. Driving up to the front door, he stopped and looked at her. "I'll be back in a few minutes."

"Are you certain you should leave me alone that long?" she asked, a little waspishly.

He leaned over and kissed her on the nose. "You're right. You do get a little cranky when you're tired. Don't worry. You'll be in bed within a half hour."

Brandi was still sputtering her response when he closed the door and went inside.

Cranky, indeed. I've been the soul of tact and diplomacy, allowing the two of them to play macho saviors.

Admit it, Brandi, you needed their help.

Maybe so, but he doesn't have to be so complacent about it.

Look, he didn't complain about your crashing his vacation, or the fact that you're now going to be his unexpected houseguest. So what's your complaint?

I don't know. I just don't like this feeling of not being in control of my life. I like to make my own decisions, do what I think best. I don't need a keeper.

Maybe not. But he certainly hasn't been overbearing or shown any dictatorial tendencies, now has he?

No. Not really. He's been very kind...and thoughtful...and caring.

Watch it. You might realize there's a great deal in the man to admire, which wouldn't do at all, now would it?

What do you mean by that crack?

Think about it.

"Oh-oh. The frown's increased even more since I left. Remind me never to keep you up past your bedtime again," Greg said, sliding under the steering wheel once again.

"I'm sorry. I was just thinking."

"In that case, spare me your thoughts. I'm not sure I could handle them this late at night."

Greg drove to the back of the motel, helped her out of the car and carried their bags inside through one of the doors. She followed him down the hallway. When he found the correct room number, he shifted the bags to one hand, inserted the key and opened the door. Then he stood back and waited for her to enter.

Brandi was surprised to find a spacious room with two queen-size beds. She walked over to the window and pulled back one of the drapes.

"I didn't ask for a room with a view. I didn't figure we'd spend much time admiring the scenery."

Brandi turned around and looked at him. He'd placed the bags on the floor and was over at the wall, adjusting the thermostat.

"I'll be a gentleman and let you have the shower first, unless you need help scrubbing your back." His gaze met hers, an expression of innocence on his face.

Brandi grabbed her bag and headed to the bathroom. "I think I can manage on my own, thank you."

"I was afraid of that," Greg said with a grin.

As soon as the bathroom door closed, Greg sat down on the side of the bed and sighed, his smile forgotten. He was trying his best not to think about the provocative situation they were in. Even though they had been alone at the cabin, this bedroom seemed to emphasize their present intimacy.

If Brandi had deliberately devised a way to torture him, she could not possibly have come up with a better method than this. However, he'd made his own decision. He had to know that she was safe. He'd rather be unable to sleep because she was only a few feet away from him than because he was concerned about her being alone.

When she came out of the bathroom, he almost groaned aloud. The soft scent she used seemed to waft around him, taunting and teasing him. He took a deep breath and stood. "Sleep well. We shouldn't be disturbed tonight."

She nodded and crossed over to the other bed, pulling back the covers without looking at him.

When she heard the door close behind him, Brandi sighed. Did Greg have any idea how difficult it was for her to continue to be this close to him night after night? She wasn't some saint without feelings. He had caused her to get in touch with emotions that she'd never known she had. Never before had she been tempted to make love.

The truth was that she knew she wanted to make love with Greg. What shocked her was the realization that she *wasn't* shocked at the thought.

She had a scary feeling that what she felt for Greg Duncan wasn't going to go away, at least not anytime soon. She kept getting sudden mental flashes of what their life together could have been like if she hadn't been so quick to turn down his proposal.

Would he want children? Brandi had never thought about having a child before, since she had never considered the possibility that she might decide to marry. Thinking about a child now seemed different, somehow. There was nothing abstract about thinking of having Greg's child—a blond-headed little girl with smoky gray eyes, or maybe a towheaded little boy with her dark blue eyes.

She shook her head, trying to dispel the images. What was the matter with her? Brandi was no longer certain that Greg had been serious, anyway. Hadn't he made a joke of his proposal with Tim? Surely he wouldn't have done that if he'd been serious.

The bathroom door opened, and she quickly closed her eyes. She'd left the bedroom lamp on so that he could find his way to his bed. Peeking beneath her lashes, Brandi discovered that Greg had tied one towel around his waist and was using another one to briskly dry his hair.

He had such a beautiful body. Her fingers itched with the longing to touch him. She must be losing her mind. How could she be wanting to touch and love this man after she'd made it clear to him that she didn't want any kind of permanent commitment with him?

The light went off, and she opened her eyes. She watched his shadowy figure crawl into bed and settle under a mound of covers.

"Good night, Greg," she whispered.

"Good night, love."

Brandi knew at that moment that there was nothing she would rather be than this man's love, if only she weren't too much of a coward to accept the challenge that he offered.

They were on their way early the next morning after having breakfast at the motel coffee shop. The weather had warmed considerably, and Brandi began to think about springtime and her plans for the craft shows.

Greg noted Brandi's absorption in her own thoughts, which suited him, since he had several things to think about. He wondered how long she would be staying with him.

He recalled that he had a trial coming up the week after next in St. Louis that he would have to prepare for.

Very seldom did he get involved in domestic-relations matters. In this case, the sister of the president of one of his corporate clients had come to him for help in getting a divorce. After hearing what she had been going through, he had decided that he could not turn her away. It was going to be a messy suit. The woman's husband was a powerful figure in the city and had strongly resisted the idea that his wife wanted a divorce. According to his wife, he had a history of being abusive to her and had a definite drinking problem. The man denied all his wife's accusations, insisting that she was hoping to blacken his reputation.

The case was going to take a great deal of preparation during the coming week, and Greg would have to go to St. Louis to try it the following week.

Would Brandi want to go with him or stay in Payton? He didn't like the idea of her staying alone, but he knew that she was chafing at the restrictions he wanted to place around her.

Greg recognized that he was at a definite disadvantage because he couldn't tell her all that Tim had related to him. As long as Tim didn't tell his colleagues Brandi's name or where she was, no government agency people would be looking for her. But what if the men now searching for her—the military—continued their search? If those men had found her in southern Colorado, they might be able to find her in Missouri.

He smiled as he thought about kidnapping her and forcing her to marry him, surprised that he could be so cavalier about the matter. As a rule, he wasn't much for fantasies, but somehow he could see him whisking Brandi away to some forgotten island, coaxing her to come be his love and share with him all the treasures that life had to offer.

Greg never noticed that the divorce case looming on his calendar had been erased from his mind and pleasurable fantasies of Brandi had taken over.

When they pulled into Greg's driveway the next afternoon, Brandi could scarcely believe her eyes. Somehow she had thought that Greg either lived in a luxury condominium or a modern, high-tech type of home. What she saw instead was a large Victorian-style house, the last thing she would have expected to find.

"What a beautiful place," she said as he helped her out of the car.

He grinned. "I'm glad you approve."

"I wasn't expecting something this large."

"I have to admit that it was an impulse buy on my part. I happened to see the For Sale sign the first time I drove the streets of Payton, not long after I had decided to move my practice here. I looked at other places, but kept returning to this house. There was such a sense of peace and permanence, as though I were a part of a family who had spent generations in the town."

They walked up the sidewalk, climbed the steps and stood on the wide porch. A swing hung at the far end, and a couple of chairs were grouped around a small round table. It looked homey and very comfortable.

The house gave Brandi an insight into Greg's character that touched her very deeply. When he opened the front door, Brandi was greeted by a wide staircase that curved to the second floor.

"I feel as though I've gone back in time. This is so beautiful. I love old homes. They have so much character."

"Yes. I feel the same way."

Brandi turned at the husky sound of his voice. The afternoon sun shone through the doorway, placing a soft glow around him and causing his light hair to shine. The casual clothes he wore in no way detracted from his appearance. Rather, they enhanced his rugged good looks.

She turned away, trying to get control of her reactions. "When do I get a tour?"

"Anytime you wish. I'll get our bags from the car."

Brandi glanced at him. "You do realize that I'm going to have to get some more clothes. I can't keep wearing these," she said, looking down at her heavy woolen pants.

"There are several shops here in town, or you can wait until next week and go with me to St. Louis."

"I didn't know you were going."

"No. I haven't mentioned it. I have a trial coming up."

"Of course. I forgot that you were a busy lawyer."

He could no longer resist the temptation. He walked over and put his arms around her. "Quite frankly, so did I. It's going to be rough getting up tomorrow and leaving you for the day."

"Greg—" She paused, uncertain of what to say. Whatever this was between them was growing stronger with every hour that passed. It scared her because she couldn't seem to hang on to any sort of control.

"I know," he said softly. "All of this is very strange to me, too. I've never felt like this about anyone. Not ever."

He leaned down and kissed her, loving the feel of her in his arms, enjoying the scent and taste of her, refusing to consider the possibility that she might not continue to be a part of his life.

"I didn't hear you come in, Mr. Duncan. I wasn't expecting you back until tonight. I told Harry this morning that—"

Brandi pulled away from Greg and peered around him. The woman who stood in the wide doorway of what appeared to be the dining room stood staring at her in shock.

"I—I'm sorry, Mr. Duncan. I thought you were alone, or I would never have—"

"That's all right, Mrs. Beasley. I'd like to introduce you to Brandi Martin. Brandi, Mrs. Beasley is kind enough to look after the place for me." He could hardly keep from laughing at the look of astonishment and curiosity on Sarah Beasley's face. "Everything looks fine, Mrs. Beasley. I really appreciate your keeping an eye on everything while I was gone."

Sarah continued to stare at him, then realized what she was doing. Her face turned a splotchy red. "Oh, that's all right. Glad to do it. I would have knocked if I'd known you were here. I just came in the back way, like I normally do. I wanted everything to be ready for you when you got in."

Her eyes kept straying to Brandi. Then she'd force her gaze back to Greg. Brandi could tell that Sarah was not used to finding Greg standing in his hallway kissing anyone. She carefully avoided meeting Greg's eyes.

"Do you live in Payton, Miss Martin?" Sarah asked.

"No. I'm just visiting."

"Yes. She'll be staying here with me."

If possible, Sarah's eyes widened even more than they had when she'd discovered Brandi's presence. Brandi almost felt sorry for the woman. She refused to make any explanations. If Greg felt it necessary, then he could make them.

He obviously didn't find it necessary, because he excused himself and went outside to get their luggage, leaving the two women standing there in the hallway.

"Well," Sarah said uncomfortably, "It's a pleasure to meet you, Miss Martin. I'm sure I'll be seeing you again."

"Probably," Brandi replied with a smile.

Sarah gave a quick nod and left the way she had come in.

When Greg returned to the house, Brandi met him at the door. "That poor woman. Couldn't you have said something to ease her curiosity?"

He laughed. "What? And attempt to curb her rampant imagination? I wouldn't think of being so cruel. I told you that this will do my reputation a world of good. The kind folk of Payton have been treating me like someone with an incurable disease ever since Penny and Brad were married. They're convinced I've been slowly pining away with a broken heart."

"I take it you don't date anyone from around here."

"No. I'm too busy to do much socializing, either here or in St. Louis."

"So my meeting you and having a chance to spend time with you was unusual."

"To be honest, I can't remember the last time I spent this much time away from work, so I suppose you're right."

"Are you going to tell Mrs. Beasley how we met?"

"Of course not. She'll have so much more fun speculating with all of her friends."

She shook her head. "You should be ashamed."

He took her by the hand and began to lead her up the stairway. "Perhaps. But I'm discovering that I rather enjoy doing the unexpected. I've lived by rules and regulations for so long that such an existence has become a habit. You showed up just in time to save me from my rut, you know. I'll be eternally grateful."

Brandi didn't know what to say. Greg paused on the landing and said, "Now you get the superdeluxe tour of my home. If you have any questions, please do not hesitate to interrupt my elaborate narrative. Refreshments will be served in the parlor directly after the tour."

His heartwarming smile enveloped her in its glow. The man was rapidly becoming irresistible. Brandi could feel her resistance to him becoming weaker and weaker.

And she didn't even care.

Chapter Nine

A week later, Brandi sat before the mirror in the guest bedroom and carefully applied makeup. Greg would be home within the hour, and he was taking her out to dinner.

Not for the first time, Brandi wondered if what she had experienced this past week was anything like marriage. If so, she could well understand why so many people were drawn to the idea.

She had come to look forward to the time when Greg would arrive home. They had fallen into a pleasant routine of sharing their experiences of the day. Brandi discovered that her days took on new meaning when she was able to report them to another person in order to once again examine what she had learned that day, either about herself or about others.

The more she was around Greg, the more she was impressed by his keen intellect. He seemed to understand her when she sometimes had trouble finding the words to describe her feelings. It was as though he were in tune with her thought patterns and able to comprehend what she was thinking.

She was also impressed by his intuitive knowledge of her, and how she must feel, having been so abruptly uprooted from her own routine and environment. He had made several suggestions that indicated he had given considerable thought to how she might wish to spend her time during the day.

There was never a doubt that she played a very large role in his thoughts even when they were apart, and she was encouraged by that fact.

One major difference between the week she had just spent and one spent married was the fact that Brandi no longer shared Greg's bed. The guest room was comfortable and she could not complain, but Brandi had discovered that sleeping with Greg had become a very pleasant habit, one that she was having trouble breaking.

She knew that she was safe and that she had only to cry out for Greg to be there by her side, checking on her. However, he never gave her any indication that he wished the relationship to progress any farther.

Had he forgotten his proposal, or was it simply that she had convinced him it was unnecessary? During this time together, neither of them had brought up any subject that could not have been discussed at a public meeting.

What Brandi had discovered was that she missed the man she'd first met, the one she'd played with in the snow, the one who couldn't seem to resist holding her... kissing her... making love to her.

She also discovered that she missed him during the day while he was gone, although she had bought a pad and pencil and had kept herself busy sketching future designs for her marquetry work. Another rather startling discovery for Brandi was that when left with no guiding thought, her pencil invariably sketched Greg in various poses. Sometimes he looked intent and serious; at other times he was laughing, his eyes filled with mischief.

She felt as though her whole body had absorbed and memorized his impression.

During the past week she had gotten into the habit of having a meal prepared and waiting for him when he got home. At first he'd explained that she didn't need to do that, but when she had insisted on trying her newfound skills in the kitchen Greg had begun to tease her about her culinary creations, which bore little resemblance to the pictures in the cookbooks.

Brandi couldn't remember a time in her life when she had enjoyed life quite so much, when she had laughed so hard, when she had so wanted to throw herself into a man's arms and plead with him to love her.

She restrained herself, of course, but she was finding it more and more difficult. As much as he teased her, and as often as she saw the softened expression he sometimes wore when he looked at her, Greg treated her with an aloof courtesy that prevented her from attempting to draw closer to him.

Not that she blamed him. His life functioned very smoothly as it was. He put in long hours at the office, Mrs. Beasley came in on a regular basis to keep his home clean, and he either made his own meals or went out to eat. Whatever he'd had in mind when he'd proposed, he wasn't looking for a housekeeper.

Brandi knew that the longer she was around him the harder it would be to adjust to being alone once again. For the first time in her life she'd discovered a person she preferred being with to being alone. What a revelation that had been.

If only she would hear something from Tim. Greg had stressed that she was not to call Tim for any reason. Tim would be in touch as soon as he knew something definite.

Tonight she had decided to do everything in her power to show Greg how much she appreciated him, how much she wanted him, how much her thinking had changed since they had first met.

The week spent in Payton had been an eye-opener. Just as Greg had predicted, by the time she had decided to go shopping everyone in town had seemed to know that she was the young woman visiting Gregory Duncan.

Brandi found the townspeople friendly and filled with carefully disguised curiosity. After several conversations with various neighbors and shopkeepers, Brandi recognized that the townspeople were proud of the fact that Greg made his home in Payton. They respected him; some revered him. To Brandi's amusement, she discovered that they all felt it their duty to warn her not to take him for granted in any way and to appreciate the sterling qualities he possessed.

Perhaps it wasn't fair to accuse the friendly folk of Payton of matchmaking. In their minds, the fact that she was actually living in Greg's home made a romance a foregone conclusion.

Brandi smiled at her image in the mirror as she put the finishing touches on her makeup. Perhaps she could prove the townspeople right in one respect, anyway. At least she was going to do her very best to remind Greg that she was a desirable woman who found him fascinating.

The phone's sudden jangling near his elbow startled Greg out of his deep concentration on the deposition he was reading. He was preparing for the Sherman dissolution hearing, which was scheduled for Monday. Otherwise he wouldn't have spent all day Saturday at the office. But he'd had no choice.

The phone rang a second time before he grabbed it. His secretary had left at noon. It was past four now.

"Hello?"

"I figured I'd find you at the office on a Saturday afternoon, even with Brandi there to keep your attention off your law books."

"Tim! It's about time you called. It's been over a week. What's taking so long?"

"I was just behaving myself, being the loyal employee whose life—and phone calls—were all legitimate and aboveboard."

"I'm impressed. What's the word?"

"Officially, nothing ever happened. Unofficially, there are a bunch of red faces in Washington, and a colonel who is getting the tail-wrenching of his life."

"You mean the colonel was working on his own?"

"You got it. What I find a little amusing—or would if Brandi hadn't been seriously threatened—is the fact that the colonel is now claiming that the men in his charge overstepped *their* authority in pursuing and threatening a witness. He denies all knowledge of the attempts on her life and swears he never extended any such authority to his men.''

Greg leaned back in his chair and smiled. ''How interesting. Perhaps he has some idea how his superiors must feel about him at the moment.''

''He probably hasn't given a thought to anything else. He's career military, and this may send him right out the door. He feels that what he was doing was justified and that eventually he will be proven right, that it's all been a misunderstanding.''

Greg leaned back in his chair. ''So where does that leave Brandi?''

''Now that the truth has come out, I admitted that I only heard about the incident through rumor. That I didn't know the person who had actually witnessed the incident.''

''And they believed that?''

Tim laughed. ''Of course they do,'' he said, his irony apparent. ''They know me so well. They also know that I don't intend to tell them anything else, and we've all agreed to drop it.''

''So Brandi's safe to return home.''

''If you want her to go, yes.''

''It isn't a case of what I want. I want Brandi to be happy, and I'm not at all sure I know how to accomplish that. She was right. I was trying to help her out of a tight situation. Now everything can return to normal.''

''Maybe you can get Brandi to accept that sort of an explanation, pal, but don't try it on me.''

Greg straightened in his chair, leaning his elbows on the desk in front of him. ''All right, so I'm a coward.

I know all about fighting to win a lawsuit. I don't know how to fight to win the woman I love."

"At least you admit that."

"Of course I do. How could anyone not love Brandi? She's so full of life, she's so unpredictable, she's so—"

"I know, I know. Then I suggest you put some of your most persuasive powers to work and win her, counselor."

Greg laughed. "I just might take your advice. I'm taking her out to dinner tonight. Do you think I should do the whole thing—candlelight dinner, romantic music and another proposal?"

"Don't ask me. That's not my line of work at all. I can save her from subversives, but not from romance."

"The only thing is, I've got a case in court in St. Louis on Monday that may take all of next week."

"So? Let her get used to seeing you in action. Take her with you."

"Are you crazy? She'll be bored out of her mind."

"I doubt that very much. I think you should give her the opportunity, anyway."

"I'll think about it."

"You do that. I've got to go. Keep in touch."

"You, too. Bye."

Greg replaced the phone slowly, his mind already reviewing all that Tim had told him.

The best news was that Brandi's life was no longer threatened. However, he'd still feel better if she agreed to marry him and move to Payton immediately. He didn't like the idea of her living all alone in such an isolated area.

He looked at the file in front of him. He needed to finish it before leaving today. Within minutes, his concentration was once again on the papers in front of him.

By the time he finished, he was determined to have his client gain her freedom from the man she'd married. She had tried several avenues to get help, but none of them had worked. The man had many problems, and it was obvious that he was refusing to face them. Instead, he was blaming everyone around him, most especially his wife.

Locking the door to his office, Greg strode to his car. He was looking forward to the evening with Brandi. Although he'd been concentrating on the case, another part of his mind had been mentally reviewing all that Tim had said.

The past week had been torture for Greg. As his guest Brandi deserved his respect. He hadn't wanted to take advantage of the situation. He hadn't wanted her to feel trapped, with no place to go. So he had given her plenty of space.

Each night he kissed her, then went to his own bedroom. He wasn't sure where he found the self-discipline to keep his hands off her. He loved her and he wanted her, and knowing she was asleep nearby was an agony that he wasn't sure he could handle much longer.

Tim's news changed things; Brandi now had a choice. She could go home, or she could stay with him, but this time the conditions would be different. He had honored her terms and treated her as a friend. Now he wanted to convince her that he wanted to add another dimension to their friendship.

When he got home, he let himself in quietly and went upstairs to shower and change. He was pleased at the way he'd managed his time since Brandi had been with him. No longer did he spend most of his waking hours at the office. Instead, he left by six each evening. If it hadn't been for this trial coming up, he wouldn't have worked today.

Greg had already started delegating some of the work in his St. Louis office by phone, knowing that he wanted to be spending more and more time in Payton. With Brandi.

Now all he had to do was to convince her to stay.

When Greg went back downstairs, Brandi was waiting.

In the time that he'd known her, he'd only seen her dressed in casual clothes. The stunning beauty waiting for him near the fireplace of his large living room stunned him.

She wore a filmy red Grecian style dress, tied at the shoulders and crisscrossed over her breasts. The skirt was full and ended at her knees. Scarlet high-heeled sandals completed the look. The bright hue played up the creaminess of her complexion and the ebony sheen of her hair.

"You look gorgeous, Brandi," he said in a husky voice.

"So do you," she managed to reply.

And he did. The black suit he had chosen to wear that night was the perfect foil for his tall, wide-shouldered figure and his bright hair. He looked commanding, arrogant and utterly luscious. Brandi swallowed, trying to rid herself of the lump that had suddenly appeared in her throat. This was the man she intended to seduce, to reduce to quivering jelly? *Her* knees felt as though they were weakening.

"Are you ready to go?" he asked.

She nodded, unable to find her voice.

He held her new coat for her, approving of the weight and length for the climate. He had teased her all week about making a career out of shopping for a new wardrobe. He'd enjoyed her showing off her latest acquisitions each day, pleased as a child who'd just discovered a new game.

She'd explained that shopping *was* new to her, that she'd never particularly cared about clothes, preferring to be casually dressed to work at home.

"I don't believe I've seen this coat or dress before, have I?" he asked, rubbing his index finger against the downy softness of her cheek.

"No. I just bought them today."

"You look lovely in them."

She smiled up at him. "I'm glad you think so."

Brandi saw such a look of warmth and caring in Greg's eyes that from that moment on the evening seemed to possess a magical quality. He made her feel beautiful and cherished and wonderful. He made her feel witty and interesting and charming.

The restaurant contributed to the mood of the evening. The tables were secluded from each other in the darkened room. A candle on each table gave additional light that seemed to leave everyone else round them in shadowy darkness—distant and unimportant to this time in Greg and Brandi's life.

Except for the occasional visit of their waiter and the wine steward, they were left alone to enjoy each other.

The music that played softly in the background called to them, and after dinner they danced to several songs. It was the first time they had ever danced together.

"Brandi?"

"Hmmmm."

"I have some news for you," Greg said, slowly circling the dance floor.

"That's nice," she murmured, enjoying being so close to him after almost a week of no more than brief good-night kisses.

"Do you want to know what it is?"

"I suppose."

"Tim called today."

That got her attention. She raised her head from where she'd been resting it on his shoulder. "What did he say?"

"That everything's been cleared up. You can go home anytime you wish."

"What was it I saw?"

"I have no idea. I doubt that you'll ever know. It's just better to forget about it and go on with your life, with one suggested change."

"What's that?"

He gazed down at her with a smile and a very vulnerable expression. "That you spend your life with me. I don't want you to go back to Colorado. Stay here and marry me."

He'd really meant it. He did want to marry her. Those were the thoughts that circled in Brandi's head.

"Oh, Greg."

He was quiet for a moment as they continued to dance to the slow music. "Is that a yes or a no?"

"I don't know what to say."

"I like that better than a no. I'll wait."

"I love you more than I've ever loved anyone in my life. It's not that—"

She couldn't say any more. His arm had tightened around her waist. She thought she heard his murmur, "Thank God," but she wasn't certain.

"Let's get out of here."

Those words were distinct and understandable. He walked her back to the table, placed money on the tray and helped her with her coat, and then they left.

The night air was crisp and clear. Hundreds of stars lighted up the sky, and Brandi lifted her face. "What a beautiful night."

"You aren't going to get off that lightly. No changing the subject." After making sure she was safely inside the car, he closed the door and walked around to the driver's side. After closing the door, he reached for her the way a hungry man reaches for a long-awaited meal.

"I love you so much," he muttered, pulling her to him. His kiss reinforced his words.

Brandi felt as though the world had suddenly exploded into a kaleidoscope of color. This kiss was not the friendly kiss he had given her each night before leaving her for the night. This kiss made leaving a sacrilege. This kiss could go on for eternity with very little effort.

When Greg finally raised his head, his face was flushed and his hair had been disarranged by Brandi's fingers.

"Let's go home," he suggested quietly.

She nodded.

When they walked into the house, neither one of them spoke. Greg slipped her coat off and hung it in the hall closet. "Would you like some coffee or something?" he asked, like a gracious host.

Brandi shook her head.

Greg led her into the living room and guided her to the sofa. As soon as she was seated he sat down beside her, taking her hands in his. "Brandi, if you aren't willing to marry me, tell me now. I have to know—Did you mean what you said earlier?"

She nodded. "I think I must have fallen in love with you the first time you kissed me, in the snow, even if I didn't realize it at the time."

"Oh, Brandi," he whispered.

Brandi felt his arms enfold her, and she felt that she was surrounded by the wonderful haven of his love. His kiss was so tender it brought tears to her eyes. How could she possibly resist this kind and sensitive man? Buried deep inside him was that young child who had never experienced unconditional love. Brandi's heart seemed to expand with a surge of feeling for him.

When he finally pulled away from her, they were both trembling. Greg's voice broke when he started to speak. He cleared his throat and in a husky tone said, "I know I'm rushing you, but I'm so afraid of losing you. I don't want to take that chance."

"I don't feel rushed at all," she admitted with a smile.

"You have no idea how badly I want to make love to you, Brandi. But I want you to be mine when I do. Can you understand that? I want our first night together to be perfect. I want to know that you want and

love me as much as I want and love you. I couldn't
bear to make love to you, then lose you."

Brandi placed her hand along his jaw. "You aren't
going to lose me, Greg. I promise."

"I've got to go to St. Louis for a trial next week. I
know I'm rushing you, but would you go with me? We
could have the judge marry us. I don't want to wait
any longer than I have already."

Brandi was aware of the tight rein he was holding on
his emotions. She knew this was important to Greg.
She didn't need the public vows and the signed document. Her commitment had already been made to
him.

However, she could better understand him since
Tim had explained about his background. His first
engagement also played an important role in how he
felt now. He didn't want a long engagement, a large
wedding, a reminder of his past.

Brandi knew that she loved him enough to agree to
whatever he wanted.

"I'll marry you, Greg. Whenever and wherever you
want."

Chapter Ten

Brandi stood in the judge's chambers and glanced around as though she were in a dream. She was becoming used to the sensation. In the past four days she had often felt as though she would wake up any minute and find herself at home, would discover that everything that had been happening to her was the result of her vivid imagination and too much rich food.

She looked across the room at the man she had met a few short weeks ago, the man she had just married. He was deep in discussion with the judge who had performed the ceremony.

Brandi focused her attention on the rings that nestled on the third finger of her left hand. The engagement ring had been placed there three days ago, the day they had arrived in St. Louis. Greg had wasted no time in starting the paperwork, arranging the blood tests and purchasing her rings.

The trial that they had come to St. Louis for had been postponed because the judge was in the midst of another trial that had run over from the week before. In fact, that trial was the topic of discussion between Greg and the judge at the moment.

Brandi almost laughed at the situation. Somehow Greg had managed to sandwich the wedding ceremony between his other appointments. How like him! If she hadn't loved him so much, she would have wanted to point out that his distracted interest in their union was not the most romantic attitude she could wish for in her groom.

But she did love him, and she wanted to be a part of his life, regardless of how much or how little of his time she shared. She knew he loved her. She also knew he had a well-organized, fully established life that had nothing to do with her. She couldn't expect him to change. She could only love him just the way he was.

Greg nodded at something the judge said, shook hands with him, then strode across the room to Brandi. He smiled as he took her arm and started toward the doorway. "Ready to go?" he asked, opening the door.

Brandi looked over her shoulder at the judge, who was already donning his robe to return to the courtroom. "Yes. Where are we going?"

He grinned. "You're asking a brand-new bridegroom where he's taking his bride? I thought I'd been too obvious to leave any doubt in your mind."

She could feel her face flush at the obvious look of desire in his face. "What about the trial?"

They came out of the courthouse and headed toward Greg's car. "The judge expects this one to be over this afternoon. Therefore ours will begin at nine in the morning."

"Don't you have to get ready for it?"

He helped her in the car. "Honey, that's all I've been doing since we got back from Colorado. I'm ready for the trial." He paused and touched her cheek lightly with his finger. "I'm also more than ready to get this marriage started."

Brandi watched as he walked around the car and got in. One thing she could say about Greg was that he had great powers of concentration. Now that he was concentrating on her, she felt that she was vibrating from the intensity of his attention.

They drove to the condominium where he stayed while in St. Louis. It was located high above the downtown area, with a view of the Mississippi River and St. Louis's famous arch.

Since they'd been in town, Greg had shown her the sights, and had taken her for a marvelous dinner at one of the restaurants located in the Union Station mall. She'd been fascinated by the artwork displayed there.

"Did you get in touch with Tim?" she asked in hopes of diffusing some of the tension that seemed to fill the car.

"I tried, but couldn't reach him."

"Then he doesn't know we're married?"

"He isn't going to be surprised. I told him when he called on Saturday that this was what I wanted."

She smiled. "And he didn't try to talk you out of it?"

"He knew better." Greg reached over and took her hand, rubbing his thumb across the rings he had placed there. "I've rushed you, haven't I?"

"I don't mind."

"But you deserved so much more—a big wedding, a white gown...."

"I'm not Penny, Greg. No matter how we would have planned it, you are the only man I've ever loved, ever wanted to marry."

He took her hand in his. "I didn't realize I was being so obvious."

"I'm sorry about the past, Greg, but I'm glad you weren't married when we met."

"So am I. It scares me to think about not having you as part of my life."

They pulled into the underground parking lot of his building, got out of the car and walked over to the elevator. Brandi glanced at her watch. "It's only two o'clock. It seems strange to have you here in the middle of the day. Are you sure there isn't something you're supposed to be doing at your office?"

He grinned. "Positive. Why do I get the feeling that you're trying to get rid of me?" They stepped into the elevator, and Greg punched the number to his floor.

She shook her head and watched the numbers of the floors they passed flash by. "I suppose I'm just nervous. I'm not really very experienced at this sort of thing."

"Neither am I. I've never been married before."

She shook her head. "I just don't want to disappoint you."

The doors opened slowly, and they stepped into the hallway. Greg already had his key out. They walked to the door in silence. After unlocking it, he motioned for her to precede him into the foyer.

They had been staying here for the last few nights. Once again, Brandi had been occupying the guest bedroom. Now she had no reason to continue to sleep alone. She turned to Greg.

"I'm being silly, I know."

"You're being adorable, as usual," he said, sliding his arms around her waist. "I apologize for my Neanderthal behavior, love. I'll admit it. All I could think about was being alone with you . . . without interruption. I didn't mean to frighten you."

Her arms crept around his neck. "I could never be frightened of you, Greg. I love you. I want to learn how to express that love. Show me how."

Never in his life had anyone looked at Greg with so much love and trust. He could feel a trembling deep within himself that he could only pray wouldn't reveal itself to her. Surely it wasn't traditionally the bridegroom who trembled.

He loved her so much. He wanted everything between them to be perfect from this day forward. Greg picked her up and carried her into his bedroom. At long last, she was where she belonged, where he had wanted her to be since the first day they had met.

Slowly he allowed her feet to touch the floor so that she was standing only a few inches from him. Then, for the first time since the wedding ceremony, Greg leaned down and kissed her.

Brandi felt as though she had been waiting for days for his kiss. Not since Saturday night had he kissed her with so much feeling, so much passion and fervor. Since coming to St. Louis he'd reverted to the chaste good-night kisses that had almost driven her out of her mind.

Now he showed no reserve whatsoever. The heat they were generating at the moment raised the temperature of the room several degrees. By the time he reluctantly raised his head, Brandi knew her knees were not going to hold her weight.

She sat down on the side of the bed and looked up at him helplessly. He knelt beside her.

"You okay?"

She nodded. His face was flushed, and his eyes glittered in the afternoon light. Without thinking, she brushed her fingers through his thick hair. Then she reached for his tie and began to loosen it.

He looked gorgeous today, the well-fitted suit contrasting beautifully with his shirt and tie. And yet all Brandi could think about at the moment was how good he looked without them. Following her instincts, she quickly unbuttoned his shirt so that she could touch his bare chest.

When her fingers touched him, she felt his reaction and her eyes met his.

Greg felt as though his heart were going to explode from its rapid beating. Brandi's touch seemed to bring his body to a quivering awareness. Quickly he shrugged out of his jacket and shirt, giving her more room to explore.

He found the zipper to her dress, slowly moving it from her neck, down her spine and to her hips. The dress fell away as though its presence were no longer necessary, the warm woolen material giving way to his masculine warmth.

In less than a minute he had Brandi totally dis-
robed and under the covers. After removing his shoes,
socks and suit pants, Greg joined her.

"This does have a certain sense of familiarity to it,
doesn't it?" he asked, pulling her into his arms.

He was right. Their bodies adjusted to each other as
though from years of habit.

"Only this time we're not asleep," Brandi managed to say, a little breathlessly.

"Were you thinking about taking a nap?" he asked,
tracing the gentle curves beneath his fingers.

"The thought never crossed my mind," she responded honestly.

"Good," he murmured with a great deal of satisfaction. Then there were no more words, unless their
soft murmurs of pleasure could be considered as such.

Greg took his time experiencing the fantasies that
had filled his head about Brandi since he'd first met
her. He kissed and caressed each and every part of her
body, coming to know her and enjoy her, revealing to
her the wonderful secrets her body had harbored while
she'd waited for the right man to come along, the man
with the right touch and the right timing to share with
her all that she needed to learn about her own sexual-
ity.

By the time Greg had moved above her, Brandi had
lost all of her self-consciousness. She had imitated his
explorations, learning his body and its responses to her
touch. Her body had taken over, eagerly awaiting each
step on the journey to fulfillment.

Greg's patience with her was rewarded. As he took
careful possession of her she relaxed and absorbed

him, accepting the natural culmination of all that they felt and shared.

Brandi marveled in the sensations she continued to experience as Greg showed her how beautiful an experience their coming together could be. He made love to her gently, but with an intensity that left no doubt that she was more important to him than anyone or anything else in his life.

Brandi felt the tension continue to mount within her as she followed his lead. Never had she experienced anything like the wonderful sensations he was evoking. She felt as though the two of them had been lifted up high above the universe to experience all that was there for two lovers to enjoy.

She let out a soft cry as her body seemed to contract and then expand, and she felt as though she were melting and becoming a part of him. Her cry seemed to be a signal to Greg, for as she held him tightly, he groaned, making one last convulsive lunge before rolling to her side and collapsing against the pillow.

So that was what lovemaking was all about, Brandi thought with a small sigh of pleasure. The complete giving of oneself to another. That intimate sharing in which hearts, minds and bodies intermingled. How could she possibly have thought that she didn't need such a sharing in her life?

Within moments they were asleep.

Streams of sunlight shone through the drapes the next morning. One fell across Brandi's face, causing her to open her eyes.

For a moment she had no idea where she was. Then she became aware of the solid warmth at her back and across her waist. Greg.

Memories of the previous day came tumbling back into her mind with clarity. They had gotten married the day before. Since then, they had spent most of their time in bed.

She glanced at the clock. It was still early. Greg had to be in court that morning, but he had plenty of time. She smiled. He needed his rest. Although they had gotten up later in the afternoon to eat, their impromptu meal had been interrupted more than once by a kiss or a caress, and they had soon found themselves back in bed.

Brandi stretched, feeling a sense of well-being that she had never before experienced. Not even her imagination had prepared her for the wonderful sense of beauty that resulted when she willingly shared herself with the person she loved.

"Good morning."

His lips touched the nape of her neck, causing her to shiver.

She shifted so that she could see his face. "Yes, it is," she said with a shy smile.

"Are you happy?"

"Extremely."

"Not sorry that I rushed you into marrying me?"

"How could I possibly be sorry about that?" She kissed him lightly, enjoying the intimacy of holding him close without the urgency of lovemaking. "What more could I possibly want in life than this?"

He glanced at his watch. "This wasn't exactly what I had in mind for a honeymoon, however."

"It doesn't matter."

"Once this trial is over, I'll clear my calendar and we'll take off, go somewhere. Wherever you want."

"I need to go home, you know. I left in such a rush. There's so much to do...pack, talk to a realtor, get my car."

"We'll do all of that. We've got all the time in the world to take care of whatever needs to be done. We're together now. That's the important thing."

"Yes," she murmured, kissing him once again.

Greg deepened the kiss and began to show her the many pleasurable sensations that could occur during lovemaking, even when there was not the urgency that had once controlled them.

Hours later, Brandi sat in the unfamiliar atmosphere of the courtroom and looked around. This was part of Greg's world, a place where he felt at home and at ease. The hushed tones of the attorneys sitting at the tables in front of the judge's bench speaking to their clients were the only sounds she heard.

There were only a couple of people sitting in the spectators' seats. Brandi smiled. She'd seen too many movies and television shows, she guessed, in which the courtroom had been filled to overflowing. The reality was much less dramatic.

She sat quietly during the morning session, not understanding any of the various motions and exhibits offered. For some reason she had thought there would be a jury, but Greg had told her that very few divorce hearings, even contested ones, had a jury.

Brandi enjoyed watching Greg at work. Now that she had seen his informal side—and his passionate side—she could better appreciate the professional who was emerging before her. She'd seen glimpses of him since they had met, but now the full force of his personality and his quiet strength seemed to take over.

She was still having trouble remembering that this man, this marvelously skilled and analytical professional, was in love with her, was married to her, was her husband.

As the days went by, she was more and more enthralled, not only by the intricacies of the law but also by the man who took her home each evening and continued showing her all the many ways a man and woman could express their love for each other.

Even now she had trouble concentrating on the case he was trying. When she watched him move between the table where his client sat and the witness chair she was reminded of the sleek muscles that were hidden beneath the suit coat he wore. When he leaned over and picked up a document she could almost feel the strength of his arms as they pulled her hard against his long, lean body.

Brandi shook her head, embarrassed that her imagination could be so active. She found the case engrossing and was determined to pay attention, and she prayed that the outcome would be all that Greg wanted.

The tension in the courtroom had steadily increased as each day had passed. Brandi felt a real compassion for Greg's client. She had been married to her husband for almost twenty years. The evidence had shown that although he was a successful businessman, his behavior at home and in private had been shocking and atrocious.

Greg glanced around the courtroom, his eye catching Brandi sitting quietly in the rear. He was pleased
with the progress of the trial. The thorough investi-
gation and careful preparation he had done on the case
had given him a decided edge, one he intended to use
to his client's advantage. He had managed to introduce enough damaging evidence against Clyde Sherman, his client's husband, to cause the man to become
obviously agitated.

Greg had hoped to show the judge the more unsta-
ble side of Sherman's nature by having the man lose
some of his composure in court.

So far, his strategy appeared to be working. During
Greg's cross-examination of Sherman, the man became increasingly flustered and irate. Although Greg
carefully kept his questions low-key, the man continued to respond in a loud and insulting manner.

After a particularly abusive outburst on Sherman's
part, the judge reprimanded him and suggested a re-
cess until Sherman could gain some control of himself.

Greg turned and walked away from the witness
stand. He glanced at his watch. It was a little after
eleven, close enough to noon that they probably
wouldn't reconvene until after lunch. He'd take Brandi
over to the little café where he liked to eat during a
trial. He was amazed that she had insisted on coming
with him each day, but pleased, too. She was taking an
active interest in his life, all phases of it. For some
reason that surprised him. But then, so much about
Brandi continued to surprise him.

Once more he glanced toward the rear of the courtroom. This time she smiled, and he returned her smile.

There was a commotion behind him, and he spun around. Sherman had left the stand, but not quietly. He was shouting obscenities and shaking his fist at Greg and at Greg's client, Carol Sherman. The bailiff was trying to quiet the man when a woman's scream rang out.

Carol Sherman shouted, "Oh, my God! He's got a gun!"

By the time Greg understood what she was screaming, he could see what the man held in his hand.

Everything seemed to move slow motion around him. Sound seemed to echo from all sides. Greg saw the man struggling with the bailiff and, for a brief moment, breaking free.

Clyde aimed the gun at the table where Greg and Carol Sherman stood and fired the pistol. Before Greg could register the events around him, he felt a heavy blow to his body, and at the same time he heard the exploding sound of the gunshot reverberating in the courtroom.

He felt no pain, just a sense of faint surprise before he lost consciousness.

Chapter Eleven

Everything happened so fast that Brandi didn't understand what was going on until she saw Greg double over and fall to the floor. Then the loud noise, the yells and the scuffling across the room began to make a horrible kind of sense.

Greg had been shot by his client's husband.

Brandi ran to the front of the courtroom, not even realizing that she was screaming Greg's name. One of the court officials caught her by the arm. "Don't crowd him, miss. We're sending for the paramedics. They should be here in a moment."

"But I've got to see him. He's got to be all right. I can't lose him now. Not now!"

She knew she wasn't making sense. Nothing in her world made sense at the moment. What was it about her that caused people to die? Was Greg going to die because he loved her? Was that why she had lost her father? And later her mother? Did she carry some sort of curse that caused the deaths of those she loved?

They wouldn't let her get near him, but one of Greg's associates, who had been sitting in on the proceedings, came over to her and guided her away when the ambulance attendants arrived.

"Mrs. Duncan? Let me drive you to the hospital. We can follow the ambulance."

She looked at him blankly.

"I'm Jack Stern, Mrs. Duncan. We met when Greg brought you to the office. Remember?"

She nodded uncertainly.

"Will you come with me?"

"I want to see Greg."

"I know you do. We'll get there as soon as we can, all right?"

The rest of the day was a blur to Brandi. People were talking all around her. Flashbulbs were going off everywhere. She vaguely remembered watching the traffic on the way to the hospital and hearing the soothing voice of Greg's associate talking to her, trying to calm her.

She felt calm. She felt numb—cut off from the world. It was her fault. She knew it was her fault. She had done this to him. She had known better. If she hadn't fallen in love with him, he would be safe.

Later she remembered them saying that he had been rushed into surgery to remove the bullet. A doctor had taken one look at her and treated her for shock. People kept asking her questions, but she didn't know how to respond. She didn't know what had happened.

When she tried to find out how badly Greg was hurt, she got only guarded replies.

Someone finally asked if she wanted anyone notified and she remembered Tim. Frantically she searched through her purse until she found his number.

She lost track of time. The doctor must have given her a sedative, because she woke up at one point and found herself lying in a quiet, shadowy room. She sat up, staring around wildly. "Greg? Where is Greg? Greg!"

A darker shadow rose from a chair beside her bed. "Try to stay calm, Mouse. I'm here."

"Tim? Oh, thank God you're here! Where is Greg? How is he? What is going on?"

"They've had Greg in surgery for several hours, love. You're going to have to be brave and hang in there."

"Oh, my God! He's going to die, isn't he? And it will all be my fault!"

Tim sat down on the bed beside her and held her close. "Your fault! What are you talking about?"

"I should never have married him. I should have known better. Don't you see? People around me die. I can't love anybody. Why didn't I remember that?"

"Brandi, get hold of yourself. You're not thinking rationally. You are not to blame for what happened today, do you hear me?" He stroked her hair. "It never occurred to anyone to search the man. So he walked right into the courtroom carrying a pistol."

"What did they do to him?"

"What they should have done before now—put him behind bars and ordered psychiatric testing. He's mad."

"That's what Greg thought, too. But he was always able to control himself around most people."

"Until now."

"But why did he shoot Greg?"

"Who knows? I personally think he was aiming for his wife. He was shouting at her, from what I can gather from the eyewitness accounts. I think Greg just happened to get in the way."

"How bad is he, Tim? Please tell me."

"I would, Mouse, if I could. I don't know anything except they've been in surgery for several hours."

"When did you get here?"

"A couple of hours ago. I chartered a jet as soon as I got the call."

She glanced around. "How long have I been in here?"

"I'm not sure. You were sound asleep when I arrived. The doctor admitted to giving you a fairly strong sedative. He said you were taking the shooting hard."

"Hard? Is that what I was doing? They wouldn't let me see him, they wouldn't tell me anything about him, I couldn't find out anything."

"I know, Mouse, I know. But I'm here now. I won't let them give you a bad time."

She felt herself relaxing against him. Thank God for Tim. What would she do without him?

They sat there quietly for a long time. Eventually Brandi stirred and said, "We've only been married a few days." She looked up at him. "Greg tried to let you know, Tim, but he couldn't reach you." She rested her head against him once again. "Neither of us wanted to wait."

Tim glanced down at her as she continued to lean against his chest. "And here I thought I was going to be part of the ceremony. Now I won't even get to be the maid of honor or the flower girl. I'm crushed."

"We'll do it again if you want. I'd be willing to do anything, if only he was going to be all right."

"Then do me a favor, will you?"

"What?"

"Stop blaming yourself because you lost your dad so young. He had a bad heart, Mouse. He knew that and he pushed himself anyway."

"But Mother always said he worked too hard to provide for us and that's what killed him."

"Brandi, your dad knew what he was doing and the chances he was taking. It was his choice. He did what he thought was best. Whether you or I agree with him is beside the point. Neither you nor your mother had anything to do with the choice he made. He loved you very much, and I know he would have hated to know that you have insisted on blaming yourself for his death all these years."

"I loved him so much, Tim." She began to cry.

"I know you did. It's all right to love him. It's even all right to miss him. But it isn't all right to limit your life because of something that happened in the past.

You couldn't change it then. You can't change it now."

"And if I lose Greg, too?"

"You're brave enough and have courage enough to accept that loss without taking the blame for it, as well. Don't try to shoulder the problems of the world, Brandi. You can love Greg without feeling responsible for him. What happened today was a freakish, totally unpredictable accident. We can't change it. We can only deal with our reaction to what has happened."

Tim was quiet for several minutes. "Greg has a real fighting spirit, Mouse. If there's any way he can, I know he'll pull through. He has so much to live for. I could see the change in him after he met you. You knocked him right off his feet, kid. He never knew what hit him. And I think you're the best thing that could ever have happened to him."

"I'm scared, Tim."

"So am I, Mouse. So am I. We've just got to leave it in God's hands now, and trust in the belief that He knows what He's doing."

There was a tap on the door, and then it opened to reveal one of the nurses.

"Mrs. Duncan?"

"Yes."

"Dr. Graham ordered a dinner tray for you. May I bring it in?"

Tim stood and answered for her. "That sounds like a great idea."

Brandi shook her head. "Oh, I don't think so. The thought of food right now—"

"Is just what you need. We can't have you in one bed and Greg laid up in another, now can we?"

Before the nurse knew what had hit her, Tim had charmed an additional tray from her. He made their meal lighthearted, keeping Brandi's mind on a multitude of subjects until she had eaten everything that had been brought to her.

Then he excused himself and left the room, promising to be back in a few minutes.

Brandi acknowledged to herself that Tim had been right. She felt better now that she had finally eaten something. She got off the bed and searched for her shoes, then went into the adjoining bathroom.

When she came back, Tim was waiting for her.

"They have Greg in Recovery. There was extensive damage that needed repair, but they feel that they did what was necessary, and he held up very well during surgery."

"Oh, thank God." Brandi burst into tears of relief. "He's going to be all right, isn't he?"

"I hope so. They said that he'll be in Recovery until morning, and they won't allow any visitors until sometime tomorrow. So how about you and me breaking out of this joint, kid, and going somewhere to get some sleep?"

Brandi was torn. She wanted to be close just in case Greg should awaken and ask for her, but Tim was no doubt right. They wouldn't allow her to see him for several hours. Despite the sleep she had gotten earlier, she knew that she needed rest. Once Greg was conscious, she wanted to spend every minute with him. She needed to prepare herself for that.

"I've got a key to the condominium. That's where we've been staying this week. We can go there." She smiled at Tim. "You'll like his place. He has a beautiful view of the river."

Tim took her arm and guided her out into the hallway. "About all I'm going to do is sleep for the next several hours, Mouse. I don't know what it is about you, but whenever I'm around you I lose sleep."

She glanced up at him and smiled. "You know, Greg was making the very same complaint this morning, over breakfast."

Tim began to laugh at the color that rose in her cheeks as she spoke. "Oh, really?" He ruffled her hair. "No doubt that's been good for him."

Her thoughts returned to the present situation, and her color faded. "He's taught me so much about loving a person." Her eyes filled with tears as they stepped into the elevator. "I can't lose him now. Not now, when I've finally found him."

Tim squeezed her hand. "Greg's not going to let anything happen to him, not if he can help it. He'll make it. Just wait and see."

Greg wasn't sure where he was. He seemed to be surrounded by a swirling gray mist. He couldn't remember why he was there. The mist seemed lighter in one direction, and he began to move toward the light.

He felt strange. Something was different, but he couldn't quite put a finger on what it was. He felt lighter, somehow, as though his body were buoyant.

Then the cloudy mist seemed to dissipate and he found himself standing in the strangest room he'd ever seen. The entire room—walls, floor and ceiling—appeared to be made up of Plexiglas. He looked down at his feet, and he could see right through the floor. The room appeared to be suspended in air. Everywhere he looked was the vast expanse of stars and the total blackness of space.

Then he saw a large round table in the center of the room. As he continued to look, a group of people appeared around the table. They glowed as though they were individually illuminated. Greg stared, trying to see their faces, but the light they projected was too bright.

"Where am I?" he asked faintly, *"And who are you?"*

One of the figures beckoned to him and said, *"Join us. It is time that you meet with the council."*

"What council? What are you talking about?"

"We are a part of your guidance group, Gregory Duncan. We have worked with you and have been with you since you were born."

"I don't understand."

"Yes, we know. Your conscious mind is unaware of our existence. It is only at night—through your dreams—that we are able to communicate with you."

"Is that what this is? A dream?"

"If you wish to view it as such. We need to confer with you to see if you are prepared to get on with your mission in life."

"My mission? I don't know what you mean."

"You have a specific lesson that you chose to work on during your lifetime, Gregory Duncan, but you have lost sight of what you wished to learn. You have

been busy working in your profession and neglecting other parts of your life.''

"I don't understand.''

"It is oftentimes easier to hide behind the duties and responsibilities of one's job rather than face the unpleasantness of growth.''

"What do you mean?''

"You have been generous with your time and your money, Gregory Duncan. It is time for you to learn to give of yourself. You talk of commitment, but you have not understood the meaning of the word. You must be willing to open up, to become vulnerable, to allow others access to your innermost feelings. You must learn to share those feelings. There is much to be done in this area.''

"I realize that. I never understood that before. Not until I met Brandi.''

"This is true. That is why we sent Brandi to you. It was time for each of you to get on with your lives, to join together and establish the family you both have secretly yearned for. It is time.''

"You mean meeting Brandi was no accident?''

"There are never any accidents, Gregory Duncan. Not even this latest one, you see. You had already grown accustomed to the idea that Brandi would fit into your life-style and that you would continue living as before. We could not have this. We understand the way your mind works, you see. Once Brandi agreed to stay with you permanently, you were already forgetting the things you had decided in Colorado to change about your life-style. This was a *reminder for you to think about these things and never to forget them."*

"What are you talking about? What has happened?"

"Don't you remember?"

"Remember what? What am I doing here?"

"You were shot, Gregory Duncan. You were shot while you were in the midst of a trial."

"I was shot. . . ."

Brandi heard the murmured words, the first coherent thing she'd heard from Greg since she'd been there. Quickly coming to her feet, she leaned over and said, "I know, darling. But you're going to be fine. The doctors all say you're recovering beautifully—"

Her voice broke on the last words, and she hastily wiped away the film of moisture that clouded her sight.

Brandi had lost track of time since Greg's shooting. She had stayed at the hospital with him as much as the doctor and nurses would allow, waiting for him to regain consciousness. Tim had gotten an emergency call that demanded his return to Denver, but he had promised to keep in as close touch as possible.

"Brandi?" Greg's voice was so faint that she could scarcely hear him.

"Yes, darling?"

"Don't leave me."

"I would never do that, believe me."

"I love you."

"I love you, too."

"I really need you in my life."

Tears poured down her cheeks, but it didn't matter. Greg had still not opened his eyes. "I need you, too."

Slowly his eyes opened. He seemed to have trouble focusing on her face. He blinked several times.

"I was shot," he repeated in a wondering tone.

"Yes."

"I had no idea they would go to such lengths to get my attention."

"Who are *they*, darling? Your client's husband was the one who shot you."

"Never mind," he murmured. "It doesn't matter." He gently stroked her hand, which lay beside his on the bed. "It worked," he said with a rueful smile. "It worked."

Two weeks later Brandi arrived at Greg's hospital room, as soon as he was allowed visitors, just as she had done each day since he'd been admitted. This time, however, he was not in bed. Instead, she found him sitting in the chair by the window.

His color was so much better. He looked more like the man she had first met. She could barely speak past the lump in her throat at the sight of him.

"Greetings, counselor," she managed to say. "You look like you're ready to practice law. All you need is a desk in front of you." She leaned over and gave him a loving, lingering kiss.

When she drew away, he grinned and said, "It's a good thing I'm no longer hooked up to those machines that monitor my heartbeat. After a kiss like that the nurses would be racing in here to see what had created such a change in my pulse."

Brandi sat down in a nearby chair and smiled at him. "Has the doctor mentioned when you might be able to leave?"

"Not exactly. He suggested we see how I do for a couple of days of limited exercise. I can now walk up and down the hallway in addition to sitting here."

Brandi shook her head. "I can't believe how differently you have reacted to your hospital stay than either Tim or I predicted."

"What do you mean?"

"We were taking bets on how long it would be before you had your secretary bringing you files and taking your dictation. Tim said he knew you'd be giving the doctor fits, demanding to be allowed to return to work."

"And you said?"

"I wouldn't take his bet. Yet here you sit without a file in sight. I'm truly amazed."

"Well, to be honest, I have been doing some business this morning. My three partners came in at my request for a short meeting."

"Oh?"

"Yes. I wanted to tell them all that I'm resigning from the firm."

Brandi stared at him in astonishment. He sat there, looking relaxed and at ease, as though he hadn't just dropped a bombshell into the conversation.

"I don't understand. Is there something about your health you haven't told me?"

"Nope. The doctor assures me there should be no lingering aftereffects of my injury and surgery. I was really very lucky."

"Then why would you resign?"

"Well, an interesting thing happened to me while I was laid up here. I discovered that I wasn't indispensable. The world is perfectly capable of running along on its own without my help."

He took her hand and cradled it between his. "When I first moved to Payton I fully intended to relinquish my practice here in St. Louis and enjoy the laid-back life-style of a small-town lawyer." He looked out the window for a moment, then returned his gaze to her. "I suppose I enjoyed being in demand, having clients insist that I handle their cases, and I allowed my work load to continue, even though I was building a practice in Payton, as well."

Studying her hand as though searching for a message, he went on. "I've had time to ask myself, 'What is the point of all of this?' and I wasn't really sure of the answer. I have all the money I need, but somehow, in the making of it, I found it easy to always want more than I had, no matter what amount that was."

Brandi knelt beside him, but she didn't say anything.

"I suppose what I'm trying to say is that I want some things in my life that money can't buy—the sound of a small child's delighted giggle, an opportunity to walk along a sandy beach with you and watch the sunset. I've had time to do a great deal of uninterrupted thinking during these past few weeks. I've been reflecting back on my childhood and teen years."

Brandi could see the shadows in his eyes when he mentioned that time in his past, but she didn't interrupt him. She knew how painful that area of his life was, even though she had never discussed it with him. Perhaps it was time for him to face that pain.

"I was thinking about what a vulnerable time in a person's life his early years are, when the need for healthy regard for yourself and your talents can make a real difference in how you turn out as an adult." His gaze met hers. "I've decided that I'd like to do something, maybe spend some time with young teenagers who might need someone to talk to once in a while, someone who remembers what it feels like to be that age. Someone who understands."

"I think that sounds wonderful, Greg. I'm sure you'll find a way to get in touch with boys in that age group once you're spending all of your time in Payton."

"I hope so." He brushed his palm across her cheek. "I also want to spend the rest of my life with you. I want us to establish a family, a warm, loving family that will provide the strong foundation for any children we might someday have."

Tears sprang to Brandi's eyes. "I can think of nothing that would please me more."

"Then you want to have children?"

"Very much, as long as they're yours."

He smiled. "Almost losing my life gave me the opportunity to see how precious and largely unappreciated my life is. Each of us is given equal amounts of time to do with as we wish. I want to enjoy my time—with you, with my family, with others that I feel an affinity for." He smiled. "Does all of this sound as though I've lost touch with my sanity?"

She shook her head. "On the contrary. It sounds extremely sane and sensible to me. And wonderful. I'm so glad you want me to be a part of it."

"A part? You are the whole of it. I would never have understood any of this if you hadn't appeared in my life. I love you so much, Brandi. It scares me to think that we might have missed meeting each other."

Brandi leaned over and hugged him. "It was only a question of time, love. I don't know how we managed not to meet before now, but we would have found each other somehow, someway. You are the other half of me. Didn't you know?"

Greg kissed her and reluctantly pulled away. "I'll be glad when I can get out of here. I seemed to have been laid up during my honeymoon. When I thought about spending the time in bed, I didn't plan on being alone!"

"We might have a slight problem, love. Tim feels that we should have another ceremony."

"Why?"

"Well, it seems that Tim was incensed that we went through a ceremony without him. He said this was the only occasion he'd ever have the opportunity in some wedding not only to give the bride away but to be the best man, as well." She grinned. "He also said that you owed the town of Payton a splashy wedding, and he for one was going to insist that you pay up."

"And how do you feel about it?"

"I don't care, so long as I'm with you. I'd repeat my vows every day of my life if necessary."

"It would be nice to have a church wedding, don't you think?"

She smiled. "I'd like that."

"So once again, Tim gets his own way." Greg shook his head and began to laugh. A less likely-looking guardian angel he'd never seen, but he had a hunch that Tim had recently earned his wings.

Epilogue

Daddy, Daddy, he's here!'' Becky cried, racing into the house and letting the screen door slam behind her. "Uncle Tim's here!"

Greg had just walked into the kitchen to see if Brandi needed any help with the lemonade and cookies she was preparing for the boys who had been helping Greg in the woodworking shop.

They turned around and looked at their five-year-old daughter, whose flyaway hair was the same color as her father's.

Greg knelt beside his oldest daughter and drew her into his arms. "Well, honey, did you invite him in, or is he still standing out on the porch?"

Becky giggled. "No. I saw his car coming, so I came to tell you."

Greg stood and took Becky's hand. "How very wise of you. Why don't we go meet him?" He glanced over his shoulder at Brandi. "He made good time, didn't he?"

Brandi grinned. "I'm not surprised. He loves my chocolate-chip cookies. I bet he locked in on them from a hundred miles out of town." She finished removing the last batch of cookies from the oven and turned. "Come on, let's go say hello, okay?"

So when Tim stepped out of his late-model sports car, he saw Greg, Brandi and Becky waiting for him at the top of the steps.

"Uncle Tim!" Becky cried, and hurled herself into his arms.

"I can't believe it," he said, catching her and hugging her to his chest. "I think you must grow an inch a week and add a pound a month! Where's the baby girl I used to bounce on my knee?"

Becky chuckled. "I'm almost ready for school now, Uncle Tim. But you can bounce Cindy if you want. She likes it, too. And she isn't so heavy."

Tim grinned at Greg and Brandi, who waited patiently for him to join them on the porch.

"I see. How heavy is she?"

Becky shrugged. "I dunno. She's still little," she said, and she held out her hands to show him.

He put her down on the porch and took Brandi in his arms. "I'm sorry I couldn't get here sooner, Mouse. But it sounds like you handled everything just fine without me."

Brandi hugged him back. "I'm just glad you made it to see us, Tim. You're looking good."

Greg threw his arm around Tim's shoulders as soon as Tim released Brandi. "Whatever you've been doing certainly seems to agree with you. I've never seen you look so rested."

They all walked into the house and, by unspoken agreement, headed for the warm, country-style kitchen.

"I decided to learn from your example, counselor. After my last assignment I decided to take some time off and just rest." He slanted a glance at Brandi. "Of course, I didn't know that Mrs. Duncan was going to get in a hurry and have the latest edition early. I wanted to be around in case you needed help with the other two." Sinking onto one of the kitchen chairs, he asked, "By the way, where are the other two members of the family?"

"Derek's taking his nap," Becky told him. "He has to take a nap because he's only three. When he's big like me he won't have to."

"I see," Tim replied with a solemn nod.

"Cindy's asleep, too. She sleeps all of the time," Becky added.

"Don't we wish," Greg said with a laughing glance at Brandi. "I'm afraid that Miss Cindy has her days and nights turned around. After her two-o'clock feeding each morning she thinks it's her place to entertain her very sleepy parents."

Tim studied Greg for a moment, then grinned. "I don't know. Fatherhood certainly does something for you. You look ten years younger than you did ten years ago."

Greg laughed. "If anyone would have told me ten years ago that I'd have three preschoolers to keep me occupied at home I would have laughed in his face."

Brandi set glasses of lemonade in front of each of them and looked at Greg. "Why don't you have Tom and Larry join us?"

Tim's brow lifted. "Tom and Larry? How did you manage to produce two more that I didn't know about?"

"They aren't ours," Brandi explained. "Well, not full-time, anyway." She looked over at Greg.

"Tom and Larry belong to my gang here in town," Greg said with a smile.

"Your gang? Like in motorcycle?"

"We're not quite that mobile, but we have a clubhouse and a charter, sweatshirts and jackets with our emblem emblazoned on the back."

"Aren't you a little old for that sort of thing, Greg?" Tim asked quizzically.

"I guess not. You see, it was my idea, and I found some young teenagers who wanted to become a part of a group. They allow me to participate because I keep the adults off their backs. In other words, I'm their token adult." He rumpled Becky's already-tousled hair and said, "And Becky's our mascot."

Greg stood and added, "I don't think the guys will want to take the time to come in right now. They've got a woodworking project they're trying to finish before the craft show next week." He picked up the second pitcher of lemonade and a plate of cookies. "I'll deliver this and be back in a minute. I'm eager to catch up on all your news, Tim."

Becky followed her father out the door, carefully carrying two glasses to hold the lemonade for Tom and

Larry. Tim looked around the kitchen with a sense of satisfaction, then smiled at Brandi.

"The place feels like home, doesn't it, Mouse?"

"It should, Tim. There's so much love in this place, I'm surprised the walls haven't burst their seams."

"I wasn't kidding earlier. Greg looks so much younger, I'm amazed."

"I know. Do you know how wonderful it is to see him so happy, so content with his life?"

"How's his law practice?"

"Busy, but he's hired two associates to help with the work load. He keeps very set hours. He has the other men do the legwork, the depositions and any investigative research that's necessary. Greg is doing more consultation work, outlining the areas that need to be dealt with and allowing the others to handle the time-consuming details."

"I don't have to ask if you're happy. You're positively glowing. I can't believe you had your third child just a few weeks ago."

She grinned. "I'm afraid I'm not glowing much in the middle of the night. I don't know what I'd do without Greg. He's so good about getting up and checking on Cindy. Once I've fed her and she's in the mood to visit, he lets me go back to sleep. He's such a loving father, Tim. It's beautiful to watch him."

"I know. There's very little resemblance to the cold and aloof man I met overseas all those years ago. Whatever the demons he was fighting, he's successfully overcome them."

Brandi heard a sound at the doorway and looked around to see Derek staring at her out of his wide silver-gray eyes.

"Where's Daddy?"

"He's out in the shop with Tom and Larry, darling. Would you like a cookie and some lemonade?"

Derek nodded and wandered into the room.

"Do you remember Uncle Tim?"

Derek's smile reminded Tim so much of Brandi's that a lump suddenly formed in his throat. He was looking at the same hair color and shape of eyes. Only the color of the eyes was different.

"Come here, sport," Tim offered, holding out his arms. Derek immediately clambered into his lap and settled there contentedly.

"You look rather natural with a child in your arms yourself, you know," Brandi pointed out with a mischievous grin.

Greg walked back into the house and paused in the doorway. Tim and Brandi had not seen him, so he had a chance to observe the scene without being noticed.

The love and affection between Tim and Brandi was apparent. Tim looked contented sitting there with Brandi's son on his lap. For a flickering of time, Greg was reminded of his fears from the past. He'd learned something very important: he didn't need to be concerned about the long-term relationship these two shared.

They had each come into his life and touched it in a very special, meaningful way. They had shown him what love was all about—how to share and become even more than who he had thought he was.

Greg remembered the years he had spent watching Brandi with their children, watching as her loving patience had spilled over to include him. They had both been so afraid at first, trying to create a marriage that would be long-lasting.

Tim had encouraged them every step of the way. And Brandi's belief in Greg when he had doubted himself at times had kept him going, even through the uncharted areas of sharing with her all that he was feeling—about himself as a man, as a father, as a guide to the young boys with whom he came into contact, as a person worthy of being loved.

Brandi had steadfastly reflected to him that he was indeed worthy.

She glanced up and saw him standing there. "Come on in, darling. We were just talking about you."

Greg forgot about the years he'd spent alone and allowed himself to rejoin their circle of love.

*   *   *   *   *

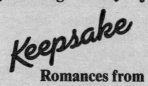

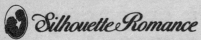

Silhouette Romance

A Trilogy by Diana Palmer

Bestselling Diana Palmer has rustled up three rugged heroes in a trilogy sure to
lasso your heart! The titles of the books are your introduction to these unforgettable men:

CALHOUN

In June, you met Calhoun Ballenger. He wanted to protect Abby Clark from
the world, but could he protect her from himself?

JUSTIN

In August, Calhoun's brother, Justin—the strong, silent type—had a second
chance with the woman of his dreams, Shelby Jacobs.

TYLER

October's long, tall Texan is Shelby's virile brother, Tyler, who teaches shy Nell
Regan to trust her instincts—especially when they lead her into his arms!

Don't miss TYLER, the last of three gripping stories from Silhouette Romance!

ATTRACTIVE, SPACE SAVING BOOK RACK

Display your most prized novels on this handsome and sturdy book rack. The hand-rubbed walnut finish will blend into your library decor with quiet elegance, providing a practical organizer for your favorite hard-or soft-covered books.

Only $9.95

Approximately 16" x 8" when assembled

Assembles in seconds!

To order, rush your name, address and zip code, along with a check or money order for $10.70* ($9.95 plus 75¢ postage and handling) payable to *Silhouette Books.*

Silhouette Books
Book Rack Offer
901 Fuhrmann Blvd.
P.O. Box 1396
Buffalo, NY 14269-1396

Offer not available in Canada.

BKR-2A

*New York and Iowa residents add appropriate sales tax.

COMING NEXT MONTH

#610 ITALIAN KNIGHTS— Sharon De Vita
Sal had been Annie's protector since she was widowed, so why hadn't he noticed how beautiful she was? She wouldn't be a widow for long—or his name wasn't Smooth, Suave Sal....

#611 A WOMAN OF SPIRIT—Lucy Gordon
Parapsychologist Dr. Damaris Sherwood thought a Victorian castle was ideal for finding a fascinating phantom. Instead, she found Boyd Radnor—ruggedly real and a man to make her spirits soar!

#612 NOVEMBER RETURNS—Octavia Street
Spunky political consultant Maggie McGraw and handsome lawyer Peter Barnes supported opposing candidates in the election, but Peter was campaigning to show her that they could win love's race—together.

#613 FIVE-ALARM AFFAIR—Marie Ferrarella
Dashing fireman Wayne Montgomery had conquered the inferno in widow Aimee Greer's kitchen, but could she take a chance and let him light a fire in her heart?

#614 THE DISCERNING HEART—Arlene James
Private maid Cheyenne Cates was hired to spy on reclusive Tyler Crawford. She never expected they would fall in love, but would she lose him when he discovered her deceit?

#615 GUARDIAN ANGEL—Nicole Monet
Self-defense instructor Alicia Mason had reluctantly agreed to marry devilish, macho Clint Kelly out of family obligation. But now her heart needed defending against his heavenly charms....

In October
Silhouette Special Edition
becomes
more special than ever
as it premieres
its sophisticated new cover!

Look for six soul-satisfying novels
every month...from
Silhouette Special Edition